King Felipe Roca de Silva y Zafiro swept in.

The door shut. Silence. Elsie wanted to berate him, but she wasn't just frozen, she was transfixed. Bereft of brain, her body was immobile. She couldn't look away and she *really* needed to.

She'd forgotten how tall he was. Tall, tense, *furious*—and staring right back at her. Through her. The intense expression in his eyes was unrelenting, unforgiving, unyielding.

Breathing got tougher. The air was hotter, thicker, and this massive room now felt small and smoky. Every emotion bubbled up to the surface—upset, hurt, isolation, longing. All of them slipped from her control. But the worst reaction was the utterly forbidden, uncontrollable *want*. King Felipe was the most handsome man she'd ever met. No, not just handsome. Handsome she could cope with. He was *compelling*—the only man to stir her into temptation. He'd roused the kind of selfish greed that had destroyed her family. He terrified her...and she was furious about it.

Elsie watched as he walked too close before he stopped. But she didn't step back. She wasn't a citizen of this country. He wasn't *her* king. And she point-blank refused to be intimidated. *Not this time.*

USA TODAY bestselling author **Natalie Anderson** writes emotional contemporary romance full of sparkling banter, sizzling heat and uplifting endings—perfect for readers who love to escape with empowered heroines and arrogant alphas who are too sexy for their own good. When she's not writing, you'll find Natalie wrangling her four children, three cats, two goldfish and one dog... and snuggled in a heap on the sofa with her husband at the end of the day. Follow her at natalie-anderson.com.

Books by Natalie Anderson

Harlequin Presents

The Greek's One-Night Heir
Secrets Made in Paradise

Once Upon a Temptation

Shy Queen in the Royal Spotlight

Rebels, Brothers, Billionaires

Stranded for One Scandalous Week
Nine Months to Claim Her

Jet-Set Billionaires

Revealing Her Nine-Month Secret

The Christmas Princess Swap

The Queen's Impossible Boss

Visit the Author Profile page
at Harlequin.com for more titles.

Natalie Anderson

THE NIGHT THE KING CLAIMED HER

Recycling programs
for this product may
not exist in your area.

ISBN-13: 978-1-335-58364-2

The Night the King Claimed Her

Copyright © 2022 by Natalie Anderson

For questions and comments about the quality of this book,
please contact us at CustomerService@Harlequin.com.

Harlequin Enterprises ULC
22 Adelaide St. West, 41st Floor
Toronto, Ontario M5H 4E3, Canada
www.Harlequin.com

Printed in U.S.A.

THE NIGHT THE KING CLAIMED HER

For Barb, Iona and Janet, aka my sorority of wise, wonderful, writerly women. You guys are central to my support system like no other and I am so grateful to have you in my life.

CHAPTER ONE

Friday, 4.05 p.m.

'LEAVE. NOW!'

A warning alarm beeped, emphasising the urgency of the harsh whisper. Elsie Wynter crunched her eyes more tightly and hunched lower in her seat. She didn't want to leave. Not again.

'Miss?' Someone spoke right above her. Someone different—a woman—not *him*. 'Miss? Please lift the window shade and ensure your safety belt is fastened.'

Elsie blinked and realised reality and nightmare had merged. She was in a plane and she *was* going somewhere new. Only they were landing far sooner than she'd expected.

'Please, miss.' The air steward shot her an authoritative glance. 'Your safety belt.'

'Of course.' Elsie followed the orders.

She always followed orders. Especially those given so seriously. But as she checked her belt she glanced at the middle-aged man across the aisle from her. 'Are we already in Spain?'

'We've been diverted,' he said softly. 'A woman on board needs medical care.'

'Oh—'

'She's having a baby a bit early but they seem

to have it under control.' The man shrugged his shoulders.

'The poor woman must be scared,' Elsie murmured.

She slid the window shade up. Their plane was moving swiftly over a vast expanse of sapphire water and a large island was rapidly coming into view. Smaller islands were visible in the distance beyond it but that main island soon swallowed the window space. Beautiful stone villas were built in the crannies of the cliffs, while to the north the island narrowed. A palace rose imposingly from the rocks at the end of the spit—like a fortress, it was a powerfully hewn beacon of strength, impervious to the ravages of weather or time or the changing needs of the world. It stood as it had for centuries. Part fortress, part palace, part medieval torture prison.

Elsie's heart pounded. She'd recognised it immediately but couldn't help asking, hoping she was wrong. Surely fate couldn't be so cruel. 'Where are we landing?'

'Silvabon.' The man peered past her. 'Beautiful, isn't it?'

Heartbreakingly beautiful, yes. She'd been here before. And in one day, one meeting—one person—had changed *everything*.

'Apparently there's a dungeon beneath that palace,' the man said. 'And treasure everywhere.'

Silvabon was a Mediterranean paradise—resplendent and timeless, a literal treasure in a vast sea.

Blessed with abundant natural resources, the kingdom had skilfully fostered strategic alliances for security—in centuries past through marriage with other royal families in the region, and in more recent times through business alliances and access to its prized shipping routes. Elsie had known they'd be flying near as they travelled from Athens to Madrid, but she'd not realised they would come this close to the illustrious kingdom—let alone be diverted directly to it.

A memory flickered—a firm step, a teasing laugh, a long look. A whisper about that dungeon. Hot hurt crescendoed as the recollection solidified. She breathed deliberately slowly to ride the worst out—humiliation and ostracism weren't strangers to her. But she'd worked too hard to let just one thought of him diminish her peace. But more than one thought of him impinged now. Elsie had spent over two months here in the glorious sunshine and luxurious atmosphere until she'd been unceremoniously evicted.

Leave. Now!

That order had come from the King himself. At the time she'd been stupidly confused why his tone had been so cruel, so urgent. She'd been more than stupid because for a second she'd thought he might actually—

No. His actions after that order had been unequivocal and utterly humiliating. So she'd not needed to be told twice and she'd vowed never to return.

But now, she rationalised with purposefully even breaths, she *wasn't* returning. Their plane was landing only to drop off the patient. The rest of the passengers—including her—wouldn't disembark. They'd simply take off again. There was no reason to be anxious.

But as they came in to land, her pulse went off beat. An army of private jets was perfectly lined up on the tarmac like a flotilla of bragging billionaire toys. Banners hung from the airport terminal and surrounding buildings. She stared at the midnight blue, black and gold—the colours of Silvabon emblazoned every possible edifice in celebration. The flags weren't fluttering. There was no wind to lift them. Because the weather was perfect. *Everything* was perfect. She knew exactly why. The mourning period for his grandfather was over and King Felipe Roca de Silva y Zafiro's official coronation was less than twenty-four hours away.

An ambulance raced to meet their plane, flanked by two fire appliances. It took only a few minutes for the distressed woman onboard to be transported away. King Felipe's people were incomparably efficient— *especially* his security team.

'Thank you for your patience and I apologise for the interruption to our journey.' The pilot spoke over the intercom. 'Unfortunately there will be further delay.'

Elsie's lungs tightened.

'We were granted permission to land only because of the medical emergency onboard. Silvabon's skies are closed for King Felipe's coronation this weekend. Because of this,' the pilot continued, 'we must remain grounded until the ceremony concludes tomorrow.'

A collective groan echoed around the plane but Elsie couldn't utter a sound.

'Can't we just take off again now?' someone called out.

'You'll be accommodated at a hotel here at the airport.' The pilot kept talking. 'Once again we apologise for the inconvenience. If you need to rebook an onward journey, our ground staff are in the terminal ready to assist.'

Elsie didn't have another plane after this one was meant to land in Madrid. She'd planned to spend the last of summer in Spain. Greece had been okay but the islands reminded her too much of Silvabon. She wanted a large city in which to become anonymous—with no views of sapphire waters. She'd find another job in another café and continue to save so she could eventually settle somewhere completely new. England, her original home, wasn't an option—there were too many desperately sad, awfully bad memories attached. But now she was back in the place she'd briefly believed to be perfect. Until the country's charmless royal had ruined everything.

Instinct urged her to hide, but surely he wouldn't find her. He wouldn't have given her a second thought after he'd booted her out of his precious country. She hadn't even said goodbye to Amalia, the one true friend she'd made here. But Amalia was the King's stepsister and after what he'd done? There'd been no chance. And that *hurt*. He'd taken too much away from her.

Elsie focused inward, calming the surging anxiety. One night in an airport hotel would be fine. No one from the palace would ever know she was here.

'Your Majesty. We have a problem.'

Not the words King Felipe wanted to hear from Major Garcia, his ageing security chief. Preparations for this wretched coronation had taken up far too much of his time already. But this was it—in less than twenty-four hours he would give his nation its ultimate royal spectacle. Pomp, ceremony, publicity. It was the first celebration in just over a decade and down to him once more. But this would be the *last* time.

'If this is the flight with the woman in preterm labour onboard, Ortiz already requested permission,' he said. 'I thought it had landed.'

'It has, Your Majesty.'

Felipe glanced up from the paperwork on his desk. 'Then what? Were the medical team unable to—?'

'She's being cared for now. The baby is premature, but all signs indicate a positive outcome.'

'Good.' Felipe looked back at the draft trade agreement he'd been perusing. 'So...'

'The other passengers onboard must stay on Silvabon until after your coronation. We could open the skies only briefly for the plane to land.'

Felipe refrained from rolling his eyes. His security was always ridiculously excessive, but they were ludicrously stringent at the moment because Felipe had not yet declared an heir. All his advisors were antsy—should Felipe meet an untimely demise they feared a war of succession as there was no close relative to take the crown. But Felipe had no intention of meeting an untimely demise and though the succession declaration rested with him, right now he was resisting it. Of course, having children of his own would provide a natural succession plan but he wasn't just resisting that. He point-blank refused. He had an alternative plan. He just needed to get through tomorrow's coronation before revealing it. The coronation had precedence over everything. So while it was unfortunate for that plane's occupants, he wasn't about to cause more stress to his team. Changing security agreements at this stage would be difficult, given so many VIPs from other countries were here. It had been a monstrous undertaking to ensure everyone's needs were met and Felipe well knew accepting inconvenience was part of palace life.

'Fortunately the flight wasn't full and we're able to accommodate the remaining passengers at a hotel,' the Major added. 'We're providing complete service for them, of course.'

Felipe nodded.

Major Garcia cleared his throat. 'Naturally we checked the passenger manifest to be sure this wasn't a possible Trojan attack.'

Felipe smothered a rueful smile. Yes, Garcia was particularly thorough at the moment. Silvabon was a constitutional monarchy but even with elected representatives forming a parliament the King—Felipe—had substantial discretionary powers far greater than similar monarchies in other countries. And poor old Garcia had already lost one royal under his watch.

'I assume no one was onboard with the intention of disrupting the coronation?' Felipe asked.

There was a momentary pause.

Felipe lifted his head to read his major's body language. The man stood unusually stiff, even for him. 'You found something?'

Wariness entered the man's eyes. 'Elsie Bailey is onboard.'

Felipe froze.

'Otherwise known as Elsie Wynter.' Garcia cleared his throat. 'She's the woman Amalia—'

'I know who she is,' Felipe clipped. His blood rushed everywhere except where he needed it most. *Elsie Wynter?*

A flash of dirty-blonde hair. A heartbeat of husky laughter. A blink of unnervingly pale blue eyes.

'She was on the flight but the plane wasn't supposed to land here?' He gritted his teeth at his roughened voice.

Garcia nodded. 'The flight was bound for Madrid.'

Felipe couldn't move. He shouldn't be bothered by Elsie Wynter's unscheduled, unintentional arrival. She wasn't here for any reason other than fate. He'd ignore it.

'Is she travelling alone?' Why had he asked that? Why did it matter?

'Yes, sir.'

His gut tightened, squeezing something cold and undeniable.

'Bring her to the palace,' he said curtly.

'Sir?'

'I want her brought to the palace. Immediately.'

The words were out before he could stop them. And they felt good.

I want her—

Fury swamped him. No. *That* wasn't why.

Elsie Wynter wouldn't escape the emotional harm she'd caused. She'd *explain*. He wanted to hear it from her damnably beautiful mouth. Why she'd vanished, why she'd let down his vulnerable stepsister, why she'd lied.

Felipe loathed liars as much as he loathed people who turned their backs on their responsibilities and *left*. Invariably those who did one, did both. Both his parents had. He wasn't having Amalia's life blighted by the same even on this minor level. She'd lost enough.

'Your Majesty—'

'High security. No drama. No witnesses,' Felipe

added uncompromisingly. 'Put Ortiz on it. Understood?'

He'd look into Elsie Wynter's cool eyes again, but he'd not be blinded by their beauty this time. It was his job to protect his young stepsister. Because of this woman, he'd failed.

For that, she would pay.

CHAPTER TWO

Three months earlier, morning

'SHE COULD BE *a security risk.'*

Felipe stiffened. He'd forgotten Ortiz, his best bodyguard, was at his side and expecting orders. Felipe resented the intrusion yet immediately castigated himself for his own distraction. He was meant to have been assessing the scene. Only in seconds he'd become entranced by the soft strumming music. He'd been straining to listen harder to that lilting voice with the husky edge that made him—

He gritted his teeth, biting back the response surging within. But now it had been acknowledged, that response became emboldened. Felipe named it with self-mockery. Desire. The woman wasn't what he'd imagined at all. She was far more—

'You really think so?' he muttered shortly.

He focused on reducing his ridiculous tension, but he'd been inadequately prepared for her beauty. Her blue and white floral dress highlighted her pale blue eyes. Slightly messy silky blonde hair framed her sweet heart-shaped face.

She looked delectable, not dangerous.

In truth Felipe's security team were too cau-

tious. His father's disappearance years ago had resulted in a deeply engrained overzealous protection plan. Now Felipe barely listened to his bodyguards' mutterings. If he did, then everyone and everything would be a security risk and he'd be unable to even breathe. That was why he'd put Ortiz on Amalia. The guy was a little less over the top. Yet now they were here. Frankly it was hard to see how and why this woman could be a threat. Except just looking at her tightened every muscle in his body. Jaw aching, he forced his attention to the person sitting beside her.

Becoming sole guardian of a thirteen-year-old he'd never before met hadn't been easy. Nor was it optional. Felipe had brought his stepsister Amalia to Silvabon six months ago. Quiet and listless, she wasn't anything like he imagined a normal young teen should be. But she was still recovering from injuries, still grieving her parents. She'd suffered too much for someone her age. As this was the first social contact she'd initiated, he needed to tread carefully. Amalia wasn't royal, she didn't have the obligations and shouldn't suffer the penalties of palace life. But while she was young and vulnerable, while she was under his protection, he had to check out who she was gravitating to. His gaze drifted back. What did this woman offer Amalia?

'She usually works alone. She bakes, updates the menu sign. The café is small but popular. Her

boss turns up later to help,' Ortiz briefed him quietly. *'Her lemon cakes are really good.'*

*Oh? For some reason the thought of Ortiz tast-
ing her food scraped Felipe's bones.* He glanced
at the menu board. The specials of the day were
written with swirling artistic streaks. *A multi-tal-
ented creative, this petite blonde leaning close to
his stepsister.*

For almost the last fortnight Amalia had come
to the café for at least an hour, sometimes longer.
Felipe had thought it might be a boy she was meeting. But no, it was this shrimp of a woman with a
canvas apron covering her billowy sundress. Her
chunky work boots looked incongruous against
that floaty fabric and an assortment of silverwork
adorned her ears. The earrings sparkled in the
morning sun and made him stare harder, longer.
Which in turn made him notice the length of her
pretty neck.

So not appropriate. *He made himself count for
four—slow and controlled as if he were diving
down in deep water.*

*They were seated out the back of the café but
still in public view, strumming chords on a weird-
shaped, undersized guitar. Safe enough surely.
But seeing Amalia bent close to the blonde put
him on edge. It shouldn't. All she was doing was
showing Amalia which frets to put her fingers on.*

'She's been in Silvabon almost three months.
Amalia's been visiting these last ten days. I have

some details but haven't run a comprehensive security check yet,' Ortiz said. 'Shall I do that now, sir?'

Felipe watched her smile at Amalia in encouragement as the girl plucked the thin metal strings. 'No. Not yet. I'll find out.'

He strode forward. As Amalia's 'bossy, overbearing' stepbrother, he couldn't do a thing right. Interfering with her new routine was hardly going to help. Too bad. His number one priority was ensuring her safety.

'Amalia.' He watched her blonde companion as he spoke. 'Aren't you going to introduce me to your friend?'

He could easily ignore Amalia's resentful expression, but the shock on the woman's face was an immediate alert. Wariness widened her eyes, furthermore fierce colour swept into her cheeks. Felipe was used to people reacting to his appearance—blushing, yes; stammering, absolutely; smiling and being unable to meet his eyes, often... But this was different. She was different. Because even though her skin flushed she held his gaze—coolly, completely. Maybe Ortiz was right.

'As if you don't know who she is already,' Amalia said. 'I saw you talking with Captain Ortiz. I'm not stupid.'

No. Just sullen and impossible to engage with, let alone make happy. Felipe tensed all over again. Being a young teen stuck in Silvabon palace? He

*knew all about the resentment that could bloom
if there was no release... But he didn't know how
to make it better for Amalia and she had to understand there were risks with her new position
as a palace resident.*

'Does she know who you are?' he asked.

*Amalia's expression turned stony. 'Are you say-
ing she only wants to spend time with me because
I'm related to you? Because she doesn't know.'*

*'She knows. Everyone in this city knows who
you are.'*

*'Well, she didn't until her boss told her and we
were already friends by then.'*

*A spark of sympathetic amusement lit the wom-
an's face as she glanced at Amalia. 'Guys, I'm sitting right here.' She turned those blue eyes back
to him. 'I'm Elsie Wynter. And you're King Felipe,
Amalia's stepbrother.'*

*She didn't stand in his presence as she ought.
So there was no curtsey. No* Your Majesty. *No*
Pleased to meet you. *No fear in those stunning
eyes either.*

*But there was a slightly mocking edge to her
self-introduction. For a moment he gazed at her.
She gazed right back—measure for measure. He
wondered what she was thinking—whether she
liked what she saw of him. Suddenly there was a
dragging sensation deep in his gut, pulling him
towards her. But he didn't move an inch. He'd met
many beautiful women in his life, he wasn't about*

to lose his equanimity here. Instead he watched and he waited. And then he saw it—the resignation flickering in her eyes. She didn't drop her gaze, but the defiant strength of it? That flatlined.

She expected him to dismiss her from Amalia's life—because she thought he knew something about her, that he'd had a security briefing? If she thought that, then there must be an element of threat. His curiosity spiked—what, why, and how?

'Amalia's been spending time with you.' He gritted his teeth, annoyingly aware he sounded like a puffed-up, overprotective older brother. Which, admittedly, was what he was. He had to be.

'I'm sitting right here, Felipe.' Amalia rolled her eyes as she echoed Elsie Wynter's light sass.

'And it's time you weren't,' he replied coolly. 'You're late for your physio. It's rude to keep your therapist waiting.'

Amalia sighed. 'So you've come to drag me back to prison?'

'Prison?' Elsie interrupted Amalia's escalating tone with a laugh. 'No, don't destroy my dreams about what living in a palace is really like.'

Amalia's eyes widened and she almost smiled.

Felipe paused, absorbing his stepsister's reaction with slight shock. He hadn't seen Amalia smile much since she'd arrived. And that she saw the palace as a prison? Not good.

But now Elsie glanced up at him with that cool defiance again. 'I'm sorry, we lost track of time.'

'Amalia didn't. She ignored the messages on her phone.' He glanced pointedly at the expensive phone placed face down on the table.

'She put it on silent at my request.'

Felipe tensed. Why didn't she want Amalia using her phone?

'We didn't want to break concentration.' Elsie seemed to read his mind.

'So her tardiness truly is your fault?'

'Sure.' A shrug of her slim shoulders exposed a soupçon more skin.

He had the strongest urge to reach out and touch it and see if it was as warm and as soft as it looked.

'No—'

'It's all right, Amalia.' Felipe interrupted his stepsister. 'I understand.'

Amalia passed the instrument back to Elsie and stood up from the wooden chair with another dramatic sigh. 'He's going to warn you away now,' she said to Elsie. 'Please ignore him. We're not really even related.'

Amalia indignantly stomped past, her limp prominent. She'd recently taken to wearing her long hair down, but it didn't hide the scarlet filling her face.

Felipe gritted his teeth, unaccustomed to failure. But he was inexperienced in a relationship like this. He'd not had a sibling before. Nor had Amalia. And he was more guardian now than *brother. The girl had no companions anywhere near her own age. And this woman? She was nearer his age than Amalia's.*

He wanted to protect his stepsister from...well, everything. Which, he realised, made him very similar to his own security team. Fundamentally he simply wanted what was best for her. But he had no idea what that even was, let alone how to achieve it.

'She's definitely not stupid.' Elsie's smile was wry. 'Knows how to strike, doesn't she?'

Felipe tried to ignore the woman's creamy skin and instead got caught up in her ice-blue eyes. Her pupils widened—not from fear. She clearly wasn't intimidated by him so the unconscious response was based in something else.

'She's more vulnerable than she thinks,' he said with an honesty more blunt than usual.

Elsie nodded regretfully. 'If you don't think I know that already, then you must think I'm stupid.'

'Jury's out,' he muttered, prodding to see what other reaction he'd receive.

Sparks flashed. 'Jury?' she echoed. 'Is impartial justice actually a possibility here? I thought you were the instant judge type.'

'No.' Unable to resist, he took the seat Amalia had vacated. 'That appears to be your forte.'

Now he was closer, something gnawing within him was soothed. He caught a hint of lemon scent and his mouth watered. He clamped his jaw shut. While her eyes were glacier blue, they weren't cold. The narrowed atmosphere between them crackled.

'Who are you, Elsie Wynter?' he eventually asked. 'Why are you in Silvabon?'

'As if you haven't had me checked out already?' She nodded her chin towards the tall man standing a few metres behind him. And the other beyond.

Yes, with wires in their ears and guns under their jackets, his plain-clothes security detail were as obvious as his fully uniformed soldiers standing guard at the palace.

'I'm checking you out now,' he murmured.

He couldn't resist. He studied her far too intently for far too long. The faint mottling on her skin and the slight parting of her full lips gave her away but she defiantly held his gaze. This electricity? She felt it too.

'So what have you learned?' she asked.

That she was more beautiful than he'd have believed. That something in her attitude made him tense. Yet at the same time he felt an impossible urge to trust her. And he wanted to learn her secrets, her past, her future, what drew her laughter or tears. And her taste. The desire to discover her taste gnawed deep. None of which he could say.

But during his hesitation she paled and swallowed. Hard. His curiosity only deepened.

'I'm not going to be in the country permanently,' she suddenly said before he could answer. 'Amalia heard me playing at the back of the café

on my break. She asked me to show her my man-dolin. I said yes before I knew who she was.'

So it was a mandolin? He nodded. But he found it most interesting that her priority was to inform him that she wasn't sticking around. Was she a threat? One part of him most definitely thought so. 'But you know who she is now.'

'My boss told me the other day when he arrived early. Until then we'd been alone,' she acknowl-edged. 'We sit out the back early, when it's quiet. She's less visible. She has an officer with her, you know. In fact, she has three.'

'I do. I also know she's been visiting daily. That's why I'm here now.'

Unmistakable resentment flared in her eyes. 'Because her meeting with me is a problem?'

'That's what I'm here to decide.' He drew a breath. Personal information wasn't something he ever shared but this was different. 'Amalia's parents died in a train crash seven months ago. She was with them and was injured too. Badly.'

'Yes. She told me.'

'She did?' As far as he was aware Amalia hadn't spoken to anyone about the accident that had killed her mother and stepfather and left her with a limp that might be life-long. Certainly not him—their interactions had begun as stilted and degenerated into simply uncommunicative. So he'd engaged a tutor and a therapist. But Ama-lia hadn't confided in either of those or any other

palace staff. Elsie was the only person he'd seen her engage with much at all.

Elsie looked at him. 'I'm sorry for your loss.'

Her voice had that edge he'd heard when she'd sung before—a fragment of the tune echoed in his head and made him think of grace and sanctuary. He tensed.

His loss.

Her acknowledgement was an unexpected balm on an old wound and an irritant to it at the same time. He pushed the sympathy away. Carlos might have been his father, but Felipe hadn't seen him in more than a decade. He'd chosen to leave and Felipe had chosen not to think of him. Because Carlos had run away with his lover and her daughter to Canada and they'd never returned to Silvabon. While Felipe's mother—shamed and blamed by his grandfather, King Javier, for the marriage breakdown—had also left the palace, emotionally broken.

Felipe had become heir to the throne and recipient of his grandfather's deep focus and ironfisted instruction. Now Amalia was as alone in the palace as he'd once been and he didn't want her to suffer the—

Felipe mentally counted to ten, slowly, deliberately, pushing all that back. But he regarded Elsie Wynter as he did. Because he couldn't turn away.

She'd paused; the emotion in her clear eyes was now concern. But there was more than that empathy. There was an echo of grief that he rec-

ognised. She'd lost someone too. He wondered who and when and how and again that desire to know her almost consumed him. This sudden fascination? Not normal for him. Not okay.

Yet she was still, exuding a quiet serenity that encouraged confidences. He lowered his gaze to avoid the startling clarity of hers but got caught by her mouth. It was slightly wide and her lips were pillowy and he suddenly thought of mussed-up sheets and husky laughter. It was a thought so out of place that he flinched.

Felipe never flinched. Ever. That was when he knew Ortiz was right. She was a security risk. To his peace of mind. To his mastery over his own body. And he had to leave.

'She wants to keep learning the mandolin,' Elsie said softly, slaying his intention to go in a millisecond. 'She's extremely musical. But I'm sure you know that already.'

Actually he didn't. He'd had no idea she was even interested. When he'd first met Amalia, having flown her privately from Canada a few days after the accident, she'd been in hospital. She'd missed the rest of the school year recovering. This summer she was catching up on her studies with a private tutor and still working on her physical strength.

'You could get a music teacher to come to the palace if you don't want her out here,' Elsie suggested.

'Why can't you come?' he said before thinking.

The 'thinking' took only another millisecond anyway. Amalia needed distraction. She'd chosen Elsie, chosen this interest. Music was fine—wholesome even. If they were in the palace grounds then his overzealous security team could relax. And besides—

Elsie's lips parted, colour stained her cheeks, and the look in her eyes?

Yes. *He might be puffed up and overprotective, but he could still stun a woman into silence. He glanced at the café roster on the kitchen wall and absorbed the information with satisfaction.*

'I don't—'

'The palace is not a prison,' *he said coolly, daring her to deny him.* 'You can see if your dreams are remotely accurate.'

'I—'

'You will be met at the gate at two p.m. Don't be late.'

'But—'

'Don't disappoint her.'

Her chin lifted, mutiny flaring in her stunningly pale eyes. 'Or?'

A ripple of something stronger than satisfaction shimmered through him now. Temptation in all its colours.

'Or you'll have to answer to me.' *He couldn't resist leaning a little closer as he stood.* 'Personally.'

CHAPTER THREE

Friday, 4.48 p.m.

'Ms Wynter?'

Elsie glanced up and stiffened. It was one of the elite force who protected King Felipe.

'Do you mind if I have a quiet word?' the guard asked. He had an earpiece and no doubt a gun concealed beneath that black jacket.

She glanced at the other passengers patiently waiting in the airport arrivals lounge and tightened her grip on her mandolin case as she recognised another plain-clothes guard a short distance away. The last thing she wanted was to attract attention. Better to answer softly, as if this weren't a worry at all. 'What about?'

'If you'll follow me, there's an office…'

Conscious of an audience, Elsie nodded and followed him. Nerves proliferated. But she wasn't about to create a scene. She'd suffered too many in the past. Public humiliation? Scorn? Rejection? She'd checked those boxes in the past and she wasn't about to tick them again in front of all these people. But the moment she got in private with this guard? Her words weren't going to be quiet.

He'd referred to her as Elsie Wynter. But on her official documents she was still Elsie Bailey. Clearly someone had done their homework. But she knew that already. It was why she'd been banished the last time she was here.

The guard led her through a door marked 'airport security'. Nerves exploded now. Was he taking her to the strip-search room? But they turned left, went through another door, then another and were suddenly out on the tarmac again. The warmth of the late afternoon was balmy but Elsie shivered. Anxiety did that to a person.

A large black vehicle was parked only a foot from the door, which meant there was no way to go around it. Another 'casually' dressed guard held the rear passenger door open.

She stared. 'Where are you—?'

'Please, Ms Wynter. I assure you, you'll be kept safe.'

Kept safe? From *what*?

'It'll only take a few minutes,' he added.

Elsie saw the sideways glances from the few airport staff still on the tarmac. Holding tight to her case, she climbed in the car. Was someone else already in there? No. The back seat was all hers. Behind her the door closed. Less than a second later the car moved. Elsie put her case down and automatically fastened her seat belt. It was less than two minutes since the first guard had approached her and now she was being driven who knew where? Only her pulse skidded because she knew already. They were on the road that led straight to the palace.

Why? That was the real question.

Celebratory banners hung above the picture-post-card cobbled streets but she couldn't appreciate the beautiful villas of the abundantly wealthy nation. Not when she could see the palace looming large. It had begun its life several centuries ago, built as a fortress to protect the rulers and to imprison those who threatened their power. Over time various additions had been made until it reached peak glorious palace. But there was no getting away from its foundations—it wasn't just a prison, but a *dungeon*.

They drove through the gleaming gates. She'd never thought she'd come back, let alone be all but kidnapped like this. Her anger built at the high-handed treatment. There was only one person to blame.

'If you'll follow me,' the guard said when he opened the door.

Despite her loose-fitting jeans and cotton cropped jumper, Elsie felt hot and sticky. She blew a stray strand of hair from her face as the guard led her along the snaking passage. In the menacing, oppressive silence her temper rose. She'd not done *anything* wrong.

The guard opened the door and stood aside for her to enter. 'Please wait in here.'

Next second she was suddenly utterly alone in a vast room designed to intimidate. On her previous visit she'd been in relatively public rooms with light, luxurious decor and all modern amenities. In this room there weren't even any windows. There were high vaulted ceilings, tapestries on the walls and uncomfortable-looking wooden furniture. There were sconces for candles though the room was currently lit by that marvel of modernity, *electricity*—but it might as well be three hundred years ago when the rights of women were non-existent and one man could order everyone to do whatever he wanted. It might as well be a prison cell. In fact, Elsie decided it was one step away from a medieval torture room.

The heavy door opened again as if by magic. It wasn't. It was one of the two armed guards waiting outside. But then...

King Felipe Roca de Silva y Zafiro swept in.

The door shut. Silence. She wanted to berate him but she wasn't just frozen, she was transfixed. Bereft of brain, her body was immobile. She couldn't look away and she *really* needed to.

He wore a black suit like his security agents but, where theirs hung slightly loose to hide weapons and allow movement, his perfectly hugged the sleek lines of his fit body. His jawline was sculpted—all sharp edges. And she'd forgotten how tall he was. Tall, tense, *furious*. And staring right back at her. Through her. The intense expression in his eyes was unrelenting, unforgiving, unyielding.

Breathing got tougher. The air was hotter, thicker, and this massive room now felt small and smoky. Every emotion bubbled to the surface. Upset. Hurt. Isolation. Longing. *All* of them slipped from her control. But the worst reaction was the utterly forbidden, uncontrollable *want*. King Felipe was the most handsome man she'd ever met. Not just handsome. Handsome she could cope with. He was *compelling*—the *only* man to stir her into temptation. Not just temptation. He'd roused the kind of selfish greed that had destroyed her family. He terrified her. And *she* was furious about it.

Elsie watched as he walked too close before he stopped. But she didn't step back. She wasn't a citizen of this country. He wasn't *her* king. And she point-blank refused to be intimated. *Not this time.*

His gaze bored into her. His eyes were the deepest brown and she'd spent too long trying to decipher what he might be thinking. She'd got it wrong. Now she knew the man wasn't just impossible to read, he was very likely thinking the exact *opposite* of how he appeared. He silently scoured her for every visible detail. She was conscious she'd been in her clothes for hours, having got up early to get to the airport. Ugh—why should she care about her appearance before him? She didn't want to *care* at all.

He still didn't break the silence—too focused on scrutinising her with serious displeasure. A tremor ran through her—a visceral response to his attention. Elsie didn't have affairs, didn't have boyfriends, didn't feel lust, let alone act on it. But the moment she'd met Felipe?

'What do you want from me?' she muttered.

It wasn't what she'd meant to ask. Certainly not with a husky whisper.

His jaw tightened.

'Am I being arrested?' She stiffened, hating that her voice was still scratchy. 'Why have I been detained and dragged before you, *Your Majesty*?'

He'd not liked her calling him that before. He'd acted as if he wanted her to be 'on the same level' as Amalia, and by extension him. As if.

'You were on the flight diverted here.'

'Yes.' She lifted her chin. 'But I didn't cause some poor woman to go into labour early. It was no plot of mine, if that's what you're thinking.'

'That's not what I'm thinking.'

'Then what?'

She needed him to stop staring at her as if she were guilty of something terrible. The condemnation felt hot and prickly and rubbed everything raw. Shame hurt. She hated that he had the power to hurt her. But he was a two-faced hypocrite. He'd acted friendly and understanding and she'd actually liked him. For a second there she'd thought she might even be able to *stay*. But behind her back he'd betrayed her, revealing his clinically cold heart.

'Your armed muscle men wouldn't even tell me why I was abducted from the airport in broad daylight.'

'They didn't know why,' he explained coolly. 'They were simply following orders.'

'*Blindly* following orders. Indulging the whims of

a spoilt royal.' She glared at him. 'Being frogmarched through the airport isn't my idea of a good time.'

'Did they really cause a great scene?' His eyebrows lifted.

'Of course, they didn't. They were ruthlessly efficient in their armed *Men in Black* style.'

'And you didn't resist?' he said softly.

She hadn't resisted at all. And she hadn't exactly been frogmarched. She'd quietly followed the guy. Right now she really regretted that. But Felipe's question picked at her wounds. 'Why should that surprise you? I've done *nothing* wrong. In fact, I've only done what I was told. But you don't trust me.'

His eyes narrowed but he didn't deny it.

'Are you going to search my case in case I've a surface-to-air rocket launcher in there?' She stiffened as he edged nearer.

He took the mandolin case from her fingers and set it on the table to his side. 'My men already know what's in here. It went through an X-ray scan. So did you. You're not armed.'

Just with words. With anger.

'Elsie.'

She froze. It hurt to hear her name on his lips. As if there were an intimacy they'd shared? There *wasn't*. That was the point. He'd been charming and she'd thought he'd not just trusted her but welcomed her. Then he'd gone behind her back and wrecked her life without a second thought. Because he was used to getting anything and everything he wanted. He did as he liked without any concern for anyone else.

'How did you know I was on board?' she asked.

'It was an unusual diversion at an unusual time and the manifest was cross-checked by my security.'

'And my name was flagged?' She was hurt. Did he really regard her as such a threat? He'd asked her to leave and she had, but he'd gone ahead to wreck the rest of her life anyway.

Elsie *Wynter* wasn't listed. Elsie Bailey was. The legal name she'd never given him yet he knew anyway. Thanks to that security team again, right? Had they ripped through the tawdry secrets and shame of her past? The humiliation of the family that she'd once thought perfect, but she'd been such a sheltered *fool*—

'Has anyone else been hauled before you, or just lucky little me?' she asked bitterly.

There was a pause. 'Just lucky little you.'

'Well, as honoured as I am,' she said coldly, 'I'd like to *leave. Now.*'

CHAPTER FOUR

Three months earlier, afternoon

ELSIE MARCHED TO the imposing gates, carrying her pride and her mandolin. Who did he think he was, demanding she appear at the palace at two p.m. on the dot? All Don't be late... Don't disappoint...

The King, duh.

When he'd walked up to their table at the café this morning Elsie should've stood and curtseyed but she'd been unable to. Literally unable to. Her legs had become wet noodles. She'd been so un-prepared—even though she'd seen his photos, of course. You couldn't live on Silvabon and not know the super-popular King's face. He was like a deity who could do no wrong and the population were all stupid proud of him. Her boss had been giddy with excitement when he'd learned Amalia was now a regular customer and he'd instructed Elsie to take extra special care of her.

Of course, Elsie took care of her. But Amalia's relationship to King Felipe wasn't why.

Only in meeting him today she'd discovered he had the deepest, dreamiest brown eyes. Tall, lean, so handsome she'd been unable to stop herself staring. But there was more than physical beauty. He'd compelled every ounce of her attention and *the way he'd assessed her had made her feel as if she were the only person on the planet.*

No. She couldn't be that foolish. To develop a crush on the one king she'd ever met? The world's most popular one? Especially when she'd then seen that the guy was a bossy, overprotective control freak.

Only that was a little harsh too, wasn't it? Because she'd caught a glimpse of human beneath his stuffy layers. He cared about Amalia. The girl had been loyal, careful not to betray her stepbrother by complaining overtly to Elsie, and Elsie respected her for that. But Amalia was obviously grieving, clearly lonely and lost in a new place, knowing almost no one—least of all her stepbrother, apparently. But it seemed Felipe was worried about her. So, of course, he made demands. And doubtless he got his way in everything. It was his normal.

But she didn't expect him to be there waiting for her inside the palace gatehouse.

'Security needs to process you.' His gaze lingered on her mandolin case.

She battled the disappointment that he'd not directly looked into her eyes. When he had earlier she'd felt a surge of energy—something hot and strong that had given her the courage to gaze right back at him. And in doing so, she'd simply taken in more. He'd been like a personal charger—a bolt of vitality that could easily become addictive. But that was so fanciful, so impossible, she had to rebel against her own wayward imagination.

'Are you security this afternoon?' she asked shortly.

In his black trousers and white shirt he'd almost fit the part—except the fabric was too fine, too perfectly tailored to his body.

'Apparently so. Supervising.'

Supervising no one. They were alone. But the palace had more security machines than any international airport. Now he met her cool look with a challenge in his eyes and took the mandolin case from her.

She clenched her empty fist as she felt that surge inside. 'Do you want fingerprints and a DNA sample?' she asked. 'Haven't you done a full background check already?' Her heart thudded. Surely he had.

His gaze narrowed slightly. 'Maybe we'll get onto that later.'

'If you think I'm a danger, why are you letting me in the door?'

'I don't necessarily think you're a danger.'

'Are you worried I'll be a bad influence on her?' She shook her head. 'Because Amalia is an independent thinker.'

'I'm aware. Believe it or not, I want to encourage that. I don't have a problem if she stands up to me.'

Elsie couldn't help a sceptical laugh.

He shot her a look. 'You think I would have a problem with that?'

'I think you're used to getting your own way. Everybody does what you tell them to.'

'Judging me so soon on so little?' He suddenly smiled. 'You're right, of course. But it's the birth-right, I can't help it.'

Elsie was too stunned to reply—his smile? Heart-stopping. Another glimpse of the human hiding within the perfection.

'Tell me,' he invited. 'In what way might I think you'll be a bad influence on her?'

She shrugged, mainly to cover her inner trembling at his smile. 'Too many earrings?'

He studied them and she regretted the silly joke because he took too long and his focus was too intent. Her neck felt exposed and vulnerable and suddenly hot and she shivered at the imaginary kiss she saw in his eyes...

Dear heaven, she was going mad. She hurriedly lifted her shoulder bag onto the X-ray machine's conveyor belt. She was reading all kinds of impossible into nothing.

King Felipe lifted her mandolin case onto the conveyor behind her bag. 'This has seen better days.'

Lots of things she owned had seen better days, but she appreciated the care with which Felipe had lifted it. She had to brace her heart every time she looked at that battered case. Her father had almost destroyed it, now she kept it together only with duct tape and string. She'd get a new one eventually but finding cases the right size was almost impossible and she didn't have the funds to have one made. And all that really mattered was that the mandolin itself—which had belonged to her mother—had survived. 'It still does the job.'

'Barely.' He glanced at her. 'If you're going to tutor Amalia in the mandolin, we need to pay you.'

Elsie paused, instinctive rejection halting her heart. She did not want to be his employee. 'I'm not taking your money.'

'You wouldn't be,' he said equably, but implacably. 'You'd be being paid for your skills and expertise.'

'No, thanks, I'm here doing a favour for a friend.'

'I don't accept favours. I don't do them either.'

She shot him a death look. 'I'm not talking about you. I mean Amalia.'

'I won't owe anyone anything,' he said firmly. 'Nor will she.'

She deliberately breathed out, wondering why he was so determinedly independent. 'So every relationship is reduced to a financial transaction? Wow. That explains a lot.'

'We're not taking advantage of our status to underpay people. Or not pay them at all.'

She inhaled sharply. 'I'm not here for money.'

Not from him. The context felt false and forced and with the fraud of her father? No. She would never accept money from Felipe.

'Your time is valuable,' he said. 'You could be working right now.'

'As I believe you're aware, I've finished my shift for the day so my time is my own. I chose to spend a little of it with Amalia. Unfortunately I didn't realise the invitation included spending time with you.'

His smile flashed. 'Had enough of me already?'

'More than enough.'

His low chuckle only aggravated her more. Honestly? The sparkling sexual attraction was something she'd never experienced and it was so inappropriate. It was all in her head, right? She was embarrassingly inexperienced and couldn't be sure of what she thought she saw in his expression. He was polite, a little caustic, but that look in his eyes...

She really wanted an ocular translation app.

Never had she ever imagined she'd meet someone royal and be so irritated by them. Or that she would talk back so sharply. She didn't ever do that. She was too busy trying to stay under the radar, hoping people wouldn't bother with her enough to ask about her past, her family...because when they found out?

'Where will I find Amalia?' she asked him hurriedly.

'She should be in the music room. I'll take you to her.' He took her mandolin case before she could, but again he lifted it carefully. Somehow that made it worse—that he was careful with something so precious to her?

Floored by her response to him, she followed him almost blindly. The intensity of this attraction? It was so awkward. She needed to escape, yet that was the last thing she wanted. She wanted nearer.

She realised they were passing through seemingly never-ending palace corridors. She blinked and looked about, trying not to be overwhelmed by the high vaulted ceilings, the light frescoes and gleaming antique furniture. And what he led her to wasn't a music room, it was a full-scale concert hall and there was a gleaming grand piano centre stage.

Amalia was waiting restlessly in the wide doorway. She had her hair pulled back from her face for the first time in a few days and as she turned to face them Elsie caught a flash of sterling silver in her ears.

'Nice earrings.' Elsie smiled at her. 'They look—'

'New, Amalia?' Felipe interrupted blandly. Too blandly.

Elsie stilled as she realised with burgeoning nerves that the girl had got them pierced—just like Elsie's—and she was only just showing them to her stepbrother, her guardian, her king. Just showing them now, when Elsie was there.

Elsie glanced at Felipe warily.

'Yes. New.' Amalia stood stiffly and didn't quite meet his eyes. 'It doesn't bother you?'

Felipe shrugged. 'Not at all.'

Yet Amalia didn't seem relieved by his unperturbed reaction. 'Could I get a tattoo, then? You'd be cool with it?'

'That would be illegal at this point because you're too young.' Felipe's expression turned solemn. 'But when you're older? It's your body, Amalia. Your rules.'

Elsie's heart thudded.

Amalia stared at him for a second. 'You're so annoying.'

She turned and stomped across the room towards the stage.

Elsie couldn't suppress a sympathetic smile as Felipe watched her go with a mystified expression. Then he glanced at Elsie.

'It wouldn't have mattered what you said,' she said softly. 'She's thirteen. And she's had a hard time. It's normal to push back.'

He didn't reply and for a moment she thought she'd overstepped the mark.

But then he sighed. 'I don't want to be anyone's gaoler.'

Something tightened within Elsie. 'You're the

ultimate authority figure around here, pretty hard to avoid that.'

He glanced up at the ceiling for a second and there it was again, the glimpse of conflict and confusion, of human.

Elsie couldn't resist unbending. 'For what it's worth, boundaries are good. And I thought yours was a good response.'

'She ambushed you too, didn't she? I saw your face.' He suddenly smiled. 'You thought I was going to blame you for the earrings, but she hadn't confided in you. Which puts you in the overprotective adult camp with me.'

He was irritatingly astute and she didn't want to be bracketed with him in any kind of camp. 'What's your tattoo, then?'

He shot her a startled look.

'If it's your body, your rules...' She leaned a little closer. 'What have you got—a quote? Your favourite animal?'

'There's no tattoo.'

'No? Not even someplace private? No piercings either?' She blinked at him innocently. 'Because?'

The muscle in his jaw flexed. 'I think you know the answer already.'

'Because you're the King?' she mocked, enjoying herself immensely. 'So serious, so important. So there's one set of rules for Amalia and another for you?'

'Absolutely. But I'm the last who'll live by those rules here. Amalia doesn't. She gets her liberty.'

'But not you?' She cocked her head. 'Why can't you have the same freedom of self-expression? Don't you get to be a man—or are you only a king?'

He stepped close and she suddenly realised what a challenge she'd issued. Magnetised, she struggled to read the swirl of emotion in his eyes—aggravation? Amusement?

'What's yours?' he asked too softly. 'More to the point, where's yours? Someplace very private?'

He was so close he stole all the oxygen and she couldn't think to answer anything but honestly. 'I don't have one.'

'So you're all talk.' He laughed—a breath of light amusement. 'Barely a rebel at all.'

That was very true. 'Amalia was right,' Elsie muttered weakly. 'You're so annoying.'

She followed Amalia's flounce across the room.

By the time she braved a quick glance back the doorway was empty and her heart—no. She couldn't be disappointed by his disappearance. She definitely didn't feel it as a loss.

She turned to Amalia, who was seated at the magnificent piano. 'You must be here all day every day.'

'I didn't know this room even existed until

lunchtime today. Felipe instructed the staff to prepare it after he came to the café.'

'Oh?' Elsie drew breath, unable to get her head around the size of the labyrinthine palace.

'Felipe said he'd get any other instruments I want. I just have to let him know.'

That was pretty damn amazing of Felipe, but Elsie frowned. 'Then what have you been playing on up till now?' From their conversations at the café she knew Amalia played piano and clarinet at least.

'I haven't.' A sheen muted Amalia's eyes. 'Not for ages.'

Not since the accident?

'And Felipe didn't know you play at all?'

Amalia just shrugged.

Not until today, then.

Elsie's heart ached. The girl was so isolated. And this explained her minor explosion at Felipe just before. These see-sawing emotions were grief-based. Because music was inextricably entwined with memory and she knew Amalia's mother had been her music teacher. And to sit at a piano for the first time now? It would bring so many memories back for her. And Elsie empathised with that so very personally. Amalia sat in a tight bundle with her hands knotted in her lap. Elsie sat beside her.

'I didn't play for a long, long time after my mother died,' she admitted quietly.

There were additional reasons for that. Ones she wouldn't ever tell Amalia. But she knew grief stole joy. And she didn't want Amalia to lose her musical expression as well. It would be another grief—one too much to bear when in fact the release might help her.

'But it heals even as it hurts, I think, sometimes,' Elsie added as she got her mandolin out of the old case and tuned it to the piano. 'Why don't we start with something simple? Just a few bars. I'll join in with you, or I'll pick something?' She drew in a steadying breath and plucked a few notes of an old folk song. 'It's been a while for me too.'

It had been for ever. She didn't want that for Amalia.

But Amalia put her hands on the keys and tested a couple of chords. Then she began. Elsie accompanied her for a little bit but after several bars she stopped and simply listened to the girl. Lost for words. Lost in the music. It was something Elsie hadn't experienced in so, so long.

'You have huge talent,' Elsie whispered, utterly awed, when Amalia stopped, meaning it completely. 'I can't teach you anything.'

Because there was natural talent and there was skill and technique. There was hard work and there was a natural feel for musical expression. Amalia had it all. Every bit.

'Don't ever stop,' Elsie whispered. 'It's too important for you.'

A wan smile bloomed through Amalia's silent tears. 'It feels better.'

But it still hurt. Elsie got that. And the only thing she could do was keep Amalia company and play alongside her. As they did—as they breathed, paused, and played, the emotions veered, passed, changed. They giggled then in almost giddy relief with that hurdle of starting now overcome. Now they could savour it. Be silly with it. Love it. And go so deeply into it the tears stung again.

'You'll stay for dinner, right?' Amalia smiled as she'd finished the repetition of a piece Elsie had adored.

'Dinner?' Elsie gaped. Was it that late already?

'Naturally she will,' Felipe said from directly behind them.

Elsie spun in fright—having an emotional explosion of her own. She glared first at his feet. The man was wearing boots, yet she'd not heard him arrive. 'You shouldn't sneak up on people.' She raised her stare, attempting to laser his too-handsome face with visual disapproval. 'How long have you been listening?'

His brown eyes were intensely full of unreadable emotion. 'Dinner is the least we can offer.' He avoided her question yet made it very clear he wasn't taking no for an answer.

That new-to-her defiance rippled through her.

'I thought you were determined to pay me so you don't have to "owe me" anything.'

He sighed. 'Demonstrate some manners for once, will you? Especially in front of the teen.'

Amalia squeaked but Elsie was too far gone on the rebellious reaction he provoked within her.

'Then try asking nicely instead of answering on my behalf.' Elsie smiled not so sweetly.

He stepped forward, out of Amalia's sightline, and fixed Elsie with such a hot stare that her brain fried. It seemed she wasn't the only one having the emotional explosion.

And in the official 'devastating stare tournament' the score read: Felipe one, Elsie nil.

'Dine with us tonight, Elsie...' His smile of very adult triumph made her shiver.

Elsie gritted her teeth. She was saying no. No.

'Please,' he added.

And at that? She simply couldn't stop herself.

'I'd be delighted to, thank you.'

CHAPTER FIVE

Friday, 5.26 p.m.

ELSIE STARED AT FELIPE. Instinct warned her to run. He was a threat to *her*. But she could only watch for his reaction to her request to *leave, now*. Would he remember?

Yeah. His pupils blew. His eyes grew impossibly darker, deeper and dangerous to anyone's peace of mind. On hers there was a catastrophic impact.

'You can't leave,' he said roughly, reinforcing the fact. 'The skies are closed. There are no flights until after tomorrow's coronation. There are too many VIP guests in town. Your plane was only allowed in as a mercy mission.'

Where was the mercy for *her*? Hadn't he done enough to her already?

'So you're making an entire planeload of people stay here for *twenty-four* hours?' She glared at him. 'You don't think that's excessive? It's like being imprisoned for no reason. Or is their time and liberty not as important as yours?'

'It's a matter of security,' he said stiffly. 'Not just mine.'

'Wouldn't it be more secure if they *left*?'

'It's the advice not just of my security general, but that of my counterparts gracing me with their presence for the coronation. They will not deviate from the plan.'

'Heaven forbid one should *deviate from the plan.*' She threw her hand in the air. 'Couldn't possibly do *that.* Even when the plan inconveniences literally *everyone* else. But we commoners simply don't matter, do we?'

But as she stared at him memories slammed her. And the breathless *yearning*? The childish fantasies she'd wrought that *one* day three months ago? That she'd allowed only one day to influence her so hugely?

He was a liar. She loathed those. She would leave and this time it would be all her own idea.

'On the contrary, you all matter very much. I've been assured everyone else who was onboard is very happy with their accommodation,' he said.

'They probably wouldn't dare say otherwise for fear of retribution.'

'Fear of retribution?' he drawled. 'It's a five-star hotel. They're paying for nothing and will have a celebratory dinner tonight.'

'Wow,' she muttered sarcastically. 'Celebrating your existence, are they? When can I get back there? I won't say no to a free dinner.'

He regarded her intently, the way a cat did a mouse. A very big cat focused on a very stunned mouse who felt she'd made a wrong move. 'Oh?'

His gaze raked down her body again. Her jeans-and-cropped-cotton-jumper combo felt too hot while the chunky boots she always wore while travelling didn't give her height enough boost. She was still too short to stare him straight in the eye. Doubtless her hair was a flat mess. It had been in a ponytail but there were loose bits falling about her face, which also felt stupidly hot. She did *not* want to feel this awkward and self-conscious. And it was *his* fault.

'Why did you make me come here?' she blurted.

He stood so still—so *coiled*—that she forgot to breathe. His eye deepened in colour—darker than midnight. She drank the sight of him in—his black hair was cropped not too long, not too short. The 'perfect' king who never broke his rules, never even bent them. Consummately reliable. Dependable. Dutiful. And extremely annoying. Because he was also rigid and inflexible and once he'd decided upon a course of action? There was no changing from the plan.

He was *spoilt*.

She'd taken one look at him—*one*—and her body had decided it wanted to be his. It was so embarrassing. Resisting the temptation to lean closer was a constant battle. Humiliating given that he'd *banished* her.

He was rhythmically tapping his fingers very slightly against his trousers. One, two, three, four… She realised he was *counting*—striving for *control*? He saw the direction of her gaze and stopped.

'Aren't you going to ask after Amalia?' he asked shortly.

She sucked in a breath because that *hurt*. She'd thought about Amalia every damned day since she'd been forced to leave this country. 'Of course. How is she?'

'You walked out on her without even saying goodbye. You made a commitment to come back and didn't.'

'Of *course*, I didn't. I *couldn't*.'

She blinked back the sudden burn of tears. She didn't care who he was, he didn't get to judge her. She'd been judged by too many already and invariably they concluded she was in the wrong. But how could he accuse her of heartlessness when it was *his* doing? She would never, ever have left Amalia the way she had if it hadn't been for him.

'Why did you leave?' he asked.

'Are you kidding?' Had he forgotten what he'd said? *How* he'd said it? She glared at him. 'You *told* me to.'

His jaw tightened. 'You took that as an order to leave the country?'

'It *was* an order.'

'You know I only meant you had to leave at that moment.'

'Or?' she challenged him.

He watched her and she felt it—that pull towards him. But it was *false*.

A muscle ticced in his jaw. 'I meant then and you know it.'

He was such a liar. 'No, you didn't. Because you

made sure I wouldn't come back.' She laughed bitterly. 'You followed through.'

He frowned. 'What?'

'How was I supposed to stay here when I'd been *fired*? Some of us have to work for a living. We're not all born with palaces and crowns and pots of gold.'

'What do you mean, "fired"?'

She stared at him. '*Every* decision you make impacts on other people's lives.'

'Elsie. As far as I'm aware you just disappeared. You didn't show up when you said you would. Security then informed Amalia that you'd left the country.'

Informed Amalia. Because *Felipe* already knew. Because she wasn't going to stay, not just where she wasn't wanted, where she was doubted, but where she could no longer even work. Her boss had thought he'd found out her past and her secrets and instantly judged her. It didn't matter that she'd worked hard for him for those two months already. All those days and all that effort she'd put in had meant nothing as soon as suspicion had been raised in his mind.

'Of course, I had. You cost me my job.'

'Then you should have come to me,' he said.

'Oh, would you have fixed everything?' She narrowed her gaze on him. 'You were the one who told him! Would you have bullied my boss into taking me back? Or paid me off? No, thanks.' She shook her head. He didn't get it. He never would. The audacity of the man to blame her when he'd been the one to interfere. 'You asked about my references. They found that video.'

That hurt the most.

'*What* video?' He pinched the bridge of his nose. 'I assure you I didn't tell anyone anything.'

'*You* didn't?' And that made everything worse. 'Of course. That would be inconvenient for you to do personally.' Too minor. 'You just let your team do your dirty work for you.'

He was the very definition of spoilt and entitled, privileged and utterly uninformed.

'Look, Elsie, I don't know what video you're talking about and I did *not* have you fired.' He huffed a breath.

He was so emphatic she almost believed him.

'What's the video even of?' he demanded.

Elsie froze. He really didn't know? He really hadn't seen it? Oh. *No.*

'Forget it.' She shut down.

She could see him thinking through all kinds of possibilities. None of which would be right, but she wasn't about to open that box. Some things were too personal. Too painful. Too *precious.*

'If my men raised doubt in your employer's mind then I apologise,' he said carefully. 'And if they did, it wasn't on my instruction.'

He'd wrecked her life and didn't even realise. He'd assumed she'd skipped out with no concern for Amalia. Which told her all she needed to know that he thought about her.

She didn't know what was worse—thinking he'd had her fired or realising that he was so little interested in her he hadn't bothered finding out what had really happened. She'd just disappeared and he didn't particularly care. He was only angry on behalf of his stepsister.

She nodded. 'Okay. Well, now that's sorted, can I leave?'

'No. This misunderstanding is…' His frown was massive as he stared at her. 'You must be hungry. Airline food isn't fantastic.'

'As if you've ever flown commercial.'

'And apparently you wouldn't say no to a free dinner.' He ignored her mutter. 'So, please, attend tonight's banquet.'

She stared at him. 'Pardon?'

'You lost your job as a consequence of your association with Amalia and me. As recompense, please attend tonight's banquet.'

'Sorry, what?' Her jaw dropped. 'You think that's going to make everything better?'

'Small things can have large consequences.' He actually smiled. 'What better way to restore your reputation on Silvabon than as a guest of the royal family?'

'You mean approval by association?' What if it backfired and he was found guilty by associating with *her*? No, thank you.

'I'm not interested in restoring my reputation,' she said stiffly. Hot humiliation flooded her cheeks—that was an *impossibility*. 'I don't want anyone to know I'm here.'

His gaze narrowed. 'What happened to not saying no to a free dinner?'

'I don't think this one will be free. I think there'll be another kind of payment attached,' she said bluntly.

His voice was velvety soft. 'Does that scare you, Elsie?'

Her pulse suddenly tripled its pace. 'Absolutely. I'll likely have my head on a spike before the night is over.'

His smile flashed again. 'But I'll be there.'

'To slay the dragons for me?' She shook her head. 'Don't you understand *you're* the dragon.'

He stepped closer. Dangerously close. 'Should I breathe fire, Elsie? Is it threats you want?'

As he walked forward, she stepped back and both kept going until she was in a very small corner of the very large room. At that point she tossed her head and stared him down. Anger—energy—blooming.

'What'll you do if I say no, Felipe? Will you lock me in this dungeon of a room and throw away the key?' She half hoped he would as long as she was alone—*away* from him.

But wicked vitality gleamed in his gaze. 'Don't tempt me.'

Tempt *him*?

'Prison doesn't scare me,' she said defiantly.

'Prison?'

'You don't know my past, so you don't know *what* you're inviting into your precious banquet.' She shook her head. 'Bet you regret not reading the security report on me now...'

'On the contrary, I'm happy not to have. It means I get to investigate you all on my own. I'll skip the banquet too. I'll stay here and find out exactly what the hell is going on with you.'

'Why do you care?'

He shrugged. 'I want to know. Everything. What's on that video, Elsie?'

No. That was an infinitely worse proposition. She didn't want to open up to him in that way. She didn't open up to anyone.

'You're bored,' she said scathingly. 'It's the eve of your coronation and you're *bored*.'

'Maybe I am. Spoilt royal, at your service.' He mock-bowed. 'So, come to the banquet. Let us apologise and make amends. For the loss of your job. For "dragging" you from the airport. Plus, you can catch up with Amalia and I know you want to do that.'

His words smote her heart because, yes, *that* was the sucker punch and he knew it. She *had* felt for Amalia. She'd felt the loneliness and grief and uncertainty. And while there'd been little she'd been able to say to make anything better, they had been able to spend time in the moment with their music. But still, self-preservation sank in. And practicalities.

'It's a ridiculous notion,' she growled. 'All the seating arrangements will be done already. You can't do that to your staff.'

He really had no idea of the impact of his capricious whims.

'They're supremely capable and finding space for lucky little you will be a breeze. They won't bat an eyelid.'

'When I walk in dressed like this?' She gestured at her baggy jeans and cropped cotton jersey.

'Your luggage will arrive shortly.'

'As if I have an evening gown stuffed in there?' Didn't he realise how ridiculous his insistence she attend was? How unnecessary? 'We are *not* from the same planet, Felipe.'

His lips twitched. 'It'll be no problem to find you a suitable dress.'

'Suitable?'

'Amalia will sort you out.'

Elsie gaped. The man had *no* idea. 'Amalia's *thirteen*. While I'm only a few inches taller than her, there are other parts that—'

'She'll find you a dressmaker.' He interrupted. 'I didn't mean for you to wear one of her dresses.' He compressed his lips.

He thought this was funny?

'It would be a good distraction for her,' he added.

'So I'm a distraction?'

He drew a sharp breath. 'She would love to see you. She's been miserable.' He glanced down to the floor and then back up. 'I'm asking for your help.'

'You call this asking? I call it abduction.'

He released a growl of a laugh as he stepped closer. 'How nicely do you need me to ask, Elsie?'

How *nicely*? He was so close she could feel his heat. It was like—

No. Don't think about it. But nothing had changed. Together they bounced between antagonism and amusement and attraction. Such *attraction*. And that was the problem.

Her heart was attempting to bash through her ribs and a wall of heat enveloped her—as her stupid, foolish body quivered at its own interpretation of what he really meant.

He leaned so close it was almost a kiss. 'Say *yes*.'

CHAPTER SIX

Three months earlier, evening

FELIPE STOOD BENEATH the streaming shower jets
and spun the tap to cold. Ideally he'd have taken
a quick swim but he didn't have time. Cool down,
get back in control, carry on.

He dressed for dinner as always. The expectation had been enforced by his grandfather and
they'd maintained the routine in recent years to
try to stave off his decline. Since his passing, Felipe had continued it. Structure and stability mattered. He didn't put on a suit though. Fresh shirt,
trousers—no jacket, no tie. It was as casual as
he got with guests.

But his temperature climbed again just at the
thought of her. There was a reason he'd left the
music room. But for the same reason he'd kept
listening. He'd leaned against the wall just outside, eavesdropping. His curiosity was too strong
to resist. He'd not heard the words clearly but
he'd felt their tone—the gentle encouragement
of husky-voiced Elsie.

Then there'd been the revelation and he
couldn't have moved even if he'd tried. He'd been
blown away by Amalia. Her talent and skill? Guilt
had swiftly followed. He'd had no idea. All these

months and he'd not known, not understood something that was such a huge part of her. But of course he should have known. Her mother had been a musician, far more than the 'floozy show-girl' his grandfather—and the media—had dismissed her as.

Amalia's immediate future was his responsibility. He'd wanted to give her time to recover from her injuries here in seclusion but now he knew he'd failed her. He owed it to her to ensure she had the training, the education to fulfil the potential, the promise and the passion she clearly felt for her music. And she needed to do that away from here where they still ran articles dismissing her mother and his father. He couldn't let them compare her to them. He wouldn't let her down again.

And the supportive tones of her five-foot-two, blue-eyed, dirty-blonde companion had devastated him. Elsie's laughter? He'd not heard laughter like that in the palace walls. Ever. Nor the singing. He'd fought to resist walking back in there, knowing they'd stop if he did. So he'd closed his eyes and listened in pure torment as the place had shimmered to life. What had Elsie drawn from Amalia?

From him *too.* There wasn't the distance between King and commoner that there should be. Somehow she'd stolen in and he'd dispensed with all proper protocol. He never should have teased *her, never let her ask him any personal questions. But from the moment they'd met formality hadn't bothered to show up. Because something else was already there—something addictive and irresistible. She'd challenged, he'd sparked. Hell, even he'd laughed and he hadn't laughed in an age either.*

In all these years he'd been sure he wasn't jealous of Amalia—for his father Carlos choosing her and her mother over him. For her having that time with him and that freedom far from the palace. Felipe was fine with it. He had a privileged life and a job to do and he honestly loved his palace and his place in it even though it wasn't always perfect... But right now?

Right now he truly envied his stepsister. He wanted Elsie's attention too.

But he couldn't have it. Not how he really wanted it. So he squared his shoulders and reached for a tie.

Elsie was conscious of the eagle-eyed palace footmen as they set out the dinner dishes. Didn't Amalia and Felipe often have dinner guests? Given how stilted and awkward the initial atmosphere was, she wasn't even sure they dined together much. Elsie looked again at Felipe. He'd got changed for dinner. He was freshly shaved and his hair was still slightly damp, his shirt crisp and his tie sharp. Immaculate. Urbane. Buttoned up. And so stunning it made her grip on the cutlery weak.

She desperately focused on the food so she didn't simply stare at him. But her appetite was pathetic—even though the soup was light and delicious, the salads fresh, the steak perfectly cooked. She kept conversation Amalia-centric. It was easiest and safest that way.

'This is amazing.' She complimented the indulgent individual molten-centred chocolate cake served for dessert.

'Not as good as your lemon cake,' Amalia said loyally.

Elsie chuckled. 'That's very kind, but untrue.'

'Do you enjoy working at the café?' Felipe suddenly asked.

He'd been quiet through dinner, only occasionally commenting as she and Amalia chatted about favourite songs.

'Very much.'

'You don't worry that working with knives you'll cut your hand and not be able to play?' Felipe asked. 'I've met other musicians who wouldn't even keep sharp knives in their home.'

'I can understand that, but it's not like I have a choice.' She laughed. 'I need to earn money.'

He looked at her steadily. 'Why not do that with your music?'

'That's flattering of you to think I could, but no.' She paused. 'I don't want pressure. I'd rather *peel a sack of potatoes for my pennies and then be able to make music just for me. But Amalia's different. She's gifted.'*

He nodded thoughtfully and turned to Amalia. 'After the coronation you'll return to school, Amalia. I was thinking we should find one with a strong music programme. There are a few on the continent I can think of that might be good.'

'School?' Amalia's eyed widened, then she frowned. Heavily.

'A specialist music school would be amazing, Amalia,' Elsie said softly. 'You could learn every instrument there is.'

Amalia shook her head. 'I don't want to go back to school.'

Felipe shrugged. 'We all must do things we don't want to. That's life.'

Amalia's frown turned into a glare. 'Like you having to marry after your coronation?'

Elsie suddenly couldn't breathe. She stared at Felipe, waiting for him to laugh it off. But he didn't. He stilled.

'Who told you about that?' he asked Amalia.

'Carlos said King Javier was furious with him and now you have to marry the woman he chose for you.'

Elsie kept looking at him, hoping he'd deny it. But he was focused on Amalia, who kept eating her chocolate cake, unaware of the arrested expression in Felipe's eyes.

'He told you that?' he prompted.

Amalia nodded and reached for her glass of water. 'He said you were the only person with the strength to handle Javier's expectations.'

Something raw flashed on Felipe's face before he dropped his gaze to the table. Elsie's heart raced silly fast. Amalia hadn't realised the profound effect of her words and not only on Felipe. It was none of her business. His future had nothing to do with her. Yet she couldn't stop herself asking him.

'You really have to get married?'

He glanced at her. Now the expression in his brown eyes was sombre and steadfast.

'To a princess.' Amalia added.

A princess? Seriously?

His gaze remained locked on hers. Something sparked, swiftly suppressed.

'Like a fairy tale?' Elsie tried to tease but it didn't feel funny. 'Or a nightmare?'

'She's already been picked,' Amalia said.

Of course he'd have to marry a princess. No doubt he'd go on to have baby princes and princesses too—securing the future of Silvabon's royal family.

Felipe inclined his head. 'I made my grandfather a promise. Several, in fact.'

'And you keep your promises?' Elsie asked, battling the horrible hot feeling inside at the thought of it all.

'Of course.'

Elsie's lungs constricted. 'Does the princess in question get any say in this? Or was the decision just made for her too?'

The corner of his mouth quirked. 'You feel sorry for her?'

'Utterly.'

'But you don't feel sorry for me?' he inferred.

Elsie forced a smile. 'Why would we feel sorry for you?'

He spread his hands. 'Not getting to choose who I marry.'

'You made the promise to your grandfather. That was the choice you made.'

'Have you never wanted to please your family?'

This time Elsie stilled, trying not to show the hit the query had. 'Some things are super impossible.'

He waited, obviously trying to read her expression but Elsie tried to stay stony and not give anything away. Somehow he still saw too much.

And suddenly his demeanour softened. 'They don't like all your earrings?'

She knew he'd deliberately lightened his tone because he'd seen her inward flinch. But she was inexplicably melancholic and not for herself. The prospect of his arranged marriage seemed cold and unromantic and even though it really had nothing to do with her she couldn't seem to let it go.

'You're really going to marry for duty? Even

though your grandfather's gone?' she asked. 'He wouldn't even know if you did or didn't. You're the King now.'

'Exactly.' Felipe's expression shuttered and he sat back. 'There's no separation of the personal and the professional for me. What I am is who I am. It impacts on every area of my life. Every decision I make.'

'Yet you don't seem to have been the one to decide the detail.'

'King Javier wanted what's best for me and for the country. He knows the kind of person needed to take on this mantle.'

'This mantle? As if you're Atlas balancing the world on your shoulders?' She shook her head. 'The King thing is just a title. You're actually just a man. You should be just a man.'

'Arranged marriages are successful around the world.'

The blunt, emotionless assessment didn't suit him. Yet she knew he meant it, that he believed it.

'Plenty of love matches fail,' he added. 'My parents' marriage, for example.' He sent Amalia a small smile. 'Don't worry, they were long out of love before my father met your mother.' He turned back to Elsie. 'But you disagree?'

She regarded him sadly, taking in this determined facet of him. 'Perhaps it will suit you. The two of you will do and say and wear the right things. It'll be perfect.'

His eyes narrowed slightly and she saw the flex of his jaw.

'I'm never getting married,' Amalia said with feeling.

'Not for at least a decade.' Felipe suddenly smiled and the whole world lifted. 'Then we'll see.'

Amalia shot him an outraged look.

'Just for that she'll elope at sixteen,' Elsie said slyly.

'Don't put ideas in her head,' he admonished her with an arched eyebrow. 'I knew I shouldn't have let you in the gates.'

Elsie chuckled. 'Bad influence at your service.'

'If I really thought that you wouldn't be here.'

'Stop trying to be reasonable,' she called him out, enjoying the burst back into banter. 'You're spoiling Amalia's and my need-to-rebel narrative. We already know you're an autocrat.'

Amalia giggled.

'Why do you need to rebel, Elsie?' Felipe asked.

She met his challenging stare and the brief hit of levity evaporated. The intensity was back and bigger than ever.

Truthfully, she didn't need to rebel. Truthfully, she wanted to fit in and be accepted like most people. But when new acquaintances or colleagues learned about her family's behaviour, they then expected the worst from her. So when they found out, she left. Living in fear of that constant judgement was like waiting for the axe to fall. It was only a matter of time. But her response to Felipe was different all over again. Absolutely—incomprehensibly—she instinctively rebelled against him. She was flint, he stone. Sparks were guaranteed. 'I don't like being told what to do.'

'Is that right?' he muttered as if he didn't quite believe her—as if he could prove her wrong.

And with horrible hot awareness she realised he could. That there were some very specific things she would do if he told her to.

Kiss me. Touch me. Spread for me.

Heat engulfed her at that shocking last instruction—what was with her suddenly rabid imagination? What was with this awful inappropriate reaction? He would never, ever...and she wouldn't, couldn't—

She cleared her throat and turned to Amalia, trying to think of an innocuous question to get them back to safety. But she saw darkening smudges beneath Amalia's eyes—emotional shadows loomed and lingered.

'You look tired, Amalia,' Elsie said, suddenly sorry. 'I'd better get home and let you rest.'

It had been a big day for the girl. Honestly, it had been a big day for Elsie too. Bigger than she'd ever intended. The consequences of meeting Felipe?

'I'm okay,' Amalia said.

But Felipe immediately stood, a frown gather-

*ing in his eyes as he nodded to a waiting footman.
'Amalia, your maid is waiting for you.' He turned
to Elsie. 'I'll escort you to the gatehouse. You'll
return tomorrow afternoon. I'm not telling you,'
he added with a meaningful emphasis. 'That was
an invitation.'*

'You call that an invitation?'

*The smallest mocking smile softened his sud-
den solemnity. 'Please.'*

*Elsie quickly hugged Amalia and then walked
with Felipe. Swift and serious, he stayed close to
her side. While that was disturbing, she was also
relieved because the palace was insanely huge.*

*'How do you find your way around here?'
Elsie muttered, unable to contain her edginess.
She was still off-kilter knowing he was going to
marry some princess, and shocked by her fevered
reactions to him. 'Don't you get lost all the time?'*

*'You want a GPS tracker?' Felipe's drawl had
both light and dark edges and that madness flared
within her again.*

*'I feel like you'd use it as an electronic tag on
me,' she said acidly. 'I wouldn't want to take a
wrong turn and end up in the dungeon.'*

*'That would take a little more than a wrong
turn.'*

*'Are the rumours true, then?' she asked, diverted.
'There really are dungeons in the basement?'*

*His smile flashed. 'No one who sees the tor-
ture chambers lives to tell anyone about them...'*

'*So prisoners really were shipped off in the middle of the night, never to be seen again?*' She parroted one of the stories spun in the tourist shops in the city centre.

'*That hasn't happened for at least a hundred years. Though that's not to say it still couldn't happen now.*'

She only half laughed—because the thought of being bailed up in Felipe's dungeon? It was a shockingly fascinating idea.

The route took them through a large portrait hall, part of the public wing of the palace. Each enormous painting depicted various members of the royal family. Elsie slowed as they came to the more modern paintings and she couldn't resist stopping at the last and studying it. '*When?*'

'*It was my investiture. A formal ceremony to recognise me as heir to the Crown after my father left,*' he explained.

She glanced back at the previous few frames. '*There aren't any pictures of him.*'

'*He abdicated.*'

'*So that means he's not part of the family any more?*' She gazed at the previous portrait and recognised his grandfather, King Javier. '*There are none of your mother either. Doesn't she live here?*'

'*She hasn't set foot in the palace since my father left her for Amalia's mother.*'

Elsie was shocked. '*Not at all?*'

'She didn't want to shoulder the burden of my grandfather's disappointment.'

It sounded as though his grandfather was more tyrant than king. To have banished people? For their images to have been literally scrubbed from the palace? It was punitive and surely must have marked Felipe deeply. 'But what about you?'

'I guess she thought I was old enough to handle it.'

She looked again at that portrait of him in a fearsomely ceremonial robe standing alone. 'How old were you at your investiture?'

'Seventeen.'

'Young.'

'Young adult,' he amended.

'Still young to have to take on adult concerns and responsibilities.'

'You think?'

'Yeah.' She didn't just think, she knew. 'I was seventeen when my mother got her diagnosis.' And as old as she'd believed she was when she was seventeen, it wasn't old enough to handle that... and maybe not things like heavy robes and crowns and the weight of a nation either.

'Ah.' He nodded. 'I'm sorry.'

In some ways Elsie wasn't. Caring for her mother through her illness had been a privilege and she'd never ever regretted the time she'd had with her. But it had been hard. Her father had absented himself—supposedly unable to cope. Her brother had avoided it too—staying away at university. Leaving Elsie alone until almost the end when—

She breathed in. So, yeah, in some ways she felt for Felipe.

'It's not easy to lose a parent at any age,' she said huskily. It was something the three of them had in common. 'Amalia's lucky to have you now.'

His gaze dropped and he cleared his throat. 'That's the most engaged and animated I've seen her since she came to Silvabon. Thank you.'

Elsie shrugged, suddenly shy. 'Music soothes the soul.'

'It wasn't the music.'

Heat slid across her body. Inappropriate, awkward, because surely that wasn't how he'd meant the compliment. She was an over-imaginative fool.

It was a few more minutes before they got to the security room at the gatehouse. There were no guards present again. She went to the door— her escape back to the real world. But she didn't open it.

She glanced up at him. 'Amalia doesn't seem enthused about going back to school.'

'The music focus will help. I'd not known how good she is. I'd not known anything about it, honestly. But boarding school in Europe will be excellent.'

Elsie's skin prickled. 'Why boarding school?'

'I don't want her to stay here.'

His bluntness shocked her. 'Why not? She's all alone. You're all she has.'

'I'm not...' His shoulders stiffened. 'This isn't the best place for her. She'll be better off away.'

Elsie wasn't so sure. 'Were you better off?'

His expression shuttered. 'I was educated here. I only had one term at boarding school in France.'

She shouldn't pry, it wasn't her business, but she couldn't resist. 'Why only one term?'

'I was needed here. I had things to learn—more than the core subjects.'

'Crowd control? How to wave politely?' She tried to joke but it wasn't that funny because she understood all those other things had really meant the loss of any carefree youth. To have such big responsibilities so young... Pressures like that shaped a person's growth.

'Boarding school will give Amalia some freedoms she won't have here. Plus she'll have people her own age around her.'

'Not random café workers with too many earrings.' Elsie half smiled. 'But I get it, you don't want her to be burdened.'

'She's already had enough to deal with.'

He'd dealt with a lot too when he was young. All the royal stuff for a start, let alone the marriage break-up and an authoritarian grandfather King.

'I'd better get back, it's getting late.' She told herself as much as she was telling him. She put

one hand on the door—about to open it. To leave. But it was as if there were an unseen cord between them that she didn't want to sever. Not yet.

And he didn't move out of her way, nor did his intense gaze leave her face. 'You're sure you don't want me to summon a car?'

'It's a gorgeous evening, too nice not to walk.'

He nodded almost robotically, and she realised he had no idea.

'You don't get to do that, do you?' she said slowly. 'You can't walk along the city streets without security guards on either side of you and the whole world staring.'

His mouth curved. 'Are you finally feeling sorry for me?'

'You don't want my pity.'

That beautiful smile faded. 'No, I don't.'

'What do you want?'

There was a long silence. She hadn't meant it provocatively. Not consciously at least. But she had provoked. She had pulled back the veil to reveal—

'Elsie...'

His huskiness emboldened her, charging that inner rebel. 'Yes, Your Majesty?'

He stepped closer. 'Since when do you bother with my title?'

Since he stood this close. Since he made her blood sing with simply a smile. Since she'd learned he belonged to someone else and sud-

denly she was so angry—because this lust was nothing more than a fever dream. It wasn't real.

Only he leaned in. 'Are you putting me in my place?'

His place? His place here, close to her, felt so right. Yet it was wrong. Because he did belong to someone else, even though Elsie knew to her bones that was wrong too. But even if his betrothal princess didn't exist this thing between them would still be wrong. Because if he knew about her family? He obviously didn't because he wouldn't be anywhere near her if he did. But his nearness now unlocked the yearning that had been building all of the damned day.

'As if you'd stay there,' she breathed. 'You're used to doing whatever you want.'

He cocked his head. 'What I want?'

The echo. The emphasis. The ache.

She couldn't turn away from him. The storm in his eyes and tension in his body mirrored her own. It wasn't a dream. Fever, yes. But real and inescapable. It was that match—fire with fire. His breath was ragged and her heart burst. This need within her was more than skin-deep, it burned through to bone. She needed him so much closer. And there was only this—one moment where anything—the ultimate—was possible. All could be hers—

'Felipe?'

His gaze drilled into her and she was pinned

in place. There was no wall at her back, no arms holding her, but it was as if she were chained. She clutched her battered mandolin case tightly. It was the last barrier between them but she couldn't drop it. For a long moment he branded her with the heat in his gaze, the steel in his stance. And then—

'You have to go,' he snapped harshly. His words scored into her skin—raking her raw like hot claws. 'You have to leave.'

The rejection was sudden and absolute and vicious. Elsie was so stunned she couldn't answer, let alone move. Her heart stopped—swollen and vulnerable and almost bursting. He swore and when he stepped closer again that tortured expression in his eyes flared.

What she saw—what she felt*—terrified her. And he told her again. 'Leave. Now!'*

CHAPTER SEVEN

Friday, 5.38 p.m.

ELSIE GLARED UP into Felipe's eyes. 'Why are you so determined I go to your stuffy banquet? I'm not some Cinderella.' She refused to say yes to him. 'Or is this just some way for you to assuage your guilt—giving lucky little me a make-over and a special trip to the zoo as if you're my fairy godmother?'

'The zoo?' He laughed. 'You might be right about that but I'm *not* your fairy godmother.'

'No?' Unable to maintain her ground against him, Elsie rested a little weight against the wall. 'Because from where I'm standing that's a lot how it seems.'

'Oh?' He lifted his arms and placed his hands either side, bracketing her in place, and leaned closer still. 'How does it seem now?'

Elsie's heart hammered as she battled the temptation to melt against him. It was the very urge she'd run from months ago. The one she'd not wanted to remember.

Because of him she'd been sent away again, when she was the happiest she'd been in years. She'd finally found a place where people didn't know her past. Who only knew her as she was *now*. Until he'd ruined everything. Yet *he* was everything. That one day had been the most thrilling of her life. Meeting him. Discovering her *weakness* for him. The weakness she needed to resist now.

'This isn't appropriate.' Elsie swallowed. 'You're supposed to be a king. A moral leader, right?'

'You don't think kings are power-hungry selfish types who do whatever they want without consideration for anyone else?'

'You said different.' She struck where she was sure he'd feel it. 'But you're not using me to cheat on your fiancée.'

But he merely smiled. And that made her angry.

'Did you think I'd forgotten that you're engaged?' she asked.

He was marrying that beautiful princess from some Alpine country in Europe. Not that she'd searched it up in a moment of weakness or anything. It hadn't been officially confirmed but there'd been a mass of speculation in a zillion articles.

'I'm touched you remember that conversation.' He leaned closer.

She remembered *every* word from that one day.

He lifted his hand and brushed back a loose strand of her hair. 'But if I was engaged to someone else I wouldn't even be talking to you right now.'

'You're never going to speak to another woman?'

'Any other woman would be fine. Just not you.' His pupils dilated. 'But as it happens, you can relax. I'm not engaged.'

Relax? Her heart hammered and her mind spun out. She tried to focus. She'd got the archaic termi-

nology wrong. 'Betrothed, then. Are you using se-
mantics to wriggle out of this?'

'Not engaged. Not betrothed. Not getting married.' His expression tightened. 'Princess Sofia and I
have decided not to ratify the betrothal once agreed
upon by her father and my grandfather.'

She didn't want to believe him. Didn't want to
feel a sudden effervescence and a head-to-toe shiver.
'What a convenient excuse to dream up when you're
pinning me to the wall like this.'

His lips curved. 'You don't believe me?'

'It hasn't been reported on.'

That princess had been mentioned in the paper at
the airport just today. There'd been speculation as
to whether she'd be at the coronation and whether
there would be an announcement regarding any im-
minent wedding.

'You've been reading the press about me?'

'No,' she lied.

'I'm waiting until after the coronation before letting all know there'll be no wedding. I don't want it
to be a distraction from the coronation.'

Elsie struggled to absorb what he'd said. 'So she
didn't want to marry you? I can't imagine why.'

'Can't you? Your amazement flatters me.' Something softened in his eyes. 'But now you know, I'm
neither your fairy godmother, nor am I someone
else's fiancé.'

'But you *are* the king of an excessively wealthy

island nation. You're about to be crowned and cele-
brated as such. Everyone has to pay homage to you.'

'Don't fret.' His lips twisted. 'I have little desire
to *force* you to kneel before me.'

She paused, thrown by the thought of being on
her knees before him. The terrible thing was it was
a totally tempting prospect that made parts of her
tighten in anticipation. She couldn't say no to him.
That was the problem. It had been the problem all
along. He made her want all the wicked things.

He smiled knowingly and, heaven help her, she
loved seeing those cracks in the facade of the very
serious King. She'd seen them before when she'd
last been here in his kingdom.

He shifted and took her hand in his. Three months
ago they'd not touched. He'd kept his distance. She'd
kept hers. Until that last moment when even then
there'd only been a heartbeat of closeness, a breath
of agony expressed. Somehow she'd known if skin
struck skin, sparks would fly. Turned out it wasn't
sparks—it was a complete detonation and it was impossible to stifle her shiver of excitement. Of anticipation. She'd *dreamed* of him touching her like this.
But the gasp she'd just released? It was mortifying.

'Felipe…' It was meant to be a warning growl. It
was more of a pleading whisper.

Triumph fired his eyes yet there was a hint of a
deeper storminess. A hesitation that she knew went
beyond them both.

She ached. How could she have missed him so

much? She barely knew him. But that one day had changed everything. The intensity of his magnetism had terrified her. It did again now—and it ripped away the facade of blame she'd cast upon him. The fact was while he'd told her to leave, she'd had no choice but to run regardless. The truth was she'd *wanted* to flee every bit as much as he'd wanted to fling her from the palace. And she'd used his words as her excuse. That unfairness of her boss's assumption was the final thing she'd used to save herself.

'I'm only going to ask one last time, Elsie. Please come to the banquet tonight.' The quiet question melted the last of her weak resistance.

'Yes,' she whispered. 'I'll come to your wretched banquet.'

'Good.'

Felipe had to release her. He had to loosen his fingers and let her go. She wasn't saying yes to what he really wanted—*yes*, she'd follow him to his personal quarters this instant and, *yes*, together they'd forget everything for a few blissful moments. Not appropriate. Not an option. But he felt a strength of satisfaction out of all proportion to what she'd agreed to. For the first time in weeks, a sore spot was soothed.

She would come to the banquet.

'Amalia will be pleased to see you,' he said mechanically. 'And my staff will make the arrangements.'

His staff were probably going to pass out in shock. Too bad.

But the second he'd heard her name this afternoon his blood had lit. The lust hadn't burned out, it had remained simmering in the background all this time while he'd tried to ignore it. He'd been so furious when she'd disappeared that he'd not been able to bring himself to ask his team where she'd gone. Why she'd gone. He'd not wanted to admit to anyone, let alone himself, how much it had bothered him. And whether it had been because of him.

Of course it had. But not quite in the way he'd thought.

He'd shut down Amalia's questions. He'd been gruff and impatient. But he'd only needed Elsie's name on a breath to be cast back into utter captivation. And now he'd seen her again, he was lost in lust like never before. Stepping away from her was impossible. He cursed the animal drive. He'd hoped it had been scarlet-tinted glasses maxing out the attraction in hindsight. But seeing the heated challenge in her ice-blue eyes, hearing her anger? It was worse than before.

Maybe she was right and he was simply bored— or taking a second to avoid what was to come tomorrow. Maybe this was one wishful hint of rebellion before making those vows. Because it couldn't be the one thing he refused to feel—not complete lust for a woman that would make him renege on *every* other promise he'd made. He would never do that.

He was not his father—not a man who would walk out on everything he was born to do, for a woman.

Tomorrow he would honour his promise to serve his people, country, duty before anything else. Any*one* else. The truth was he already did. His life hadn't been wholly his own for a long time and despite the ceremony tomorrow not much would actually change. It was a formality, a celebration of the fundamentals that had been in place since his accession to the throne the second his grandfather had passed. This was a thing his people wanted and he couldn't deny the economic benefits of this weekend. This pinnacle positive event of the decade was going to be streamed so anyone in the world could watch. And as there was never going to be a wedding, he needed to step up for this one. He would do so with all the loyalty and love he felt towards his country and the people within.

But tonight's banquet was the 'private' event. There'd be no cameras other than those permitted in the atrium and he'd ensure no photos were taken of Amalia or her companion. He'd apologised to Elsie. He'd now ensure she was cared for tonight. And that didn't mean her ending up in his bed.

Not an option.

Because while he'd been furious that she'd walked out, he'd also been relieved. Felipe didn't often have affairs. It was difficult to maintain privacy here on Silvabon and his former betrothal had come in handy as deflection from women who wanted to get too serious. But the trigger for his final rejection of that betrothal was standing right in front of him. He couldn't consider a political alliance once he'd realised how badly he could want someone else. And while he'd once wanted to do his duty for his grandfather, he'd realised that the sacrifice wasn't only his to bear.

None of it would have been fair on Princess Sofia.

Finally he'd realised he would never ask *anyone* to move to Silvabon for him. Palace life had broken his mother. It had also broken his father—a man who'd been born into the life and had every preparation and support but who still hadn't been able to make it.

So Felipe wasn't asking anyone to take it on. Not ever.

Yet a thread of rebellion tightened within him. He'd been so good for so long—he'd done everything demanded of him. Now he wanted something for himself. Because despite Elsie's little digs to the contrary, he wasn't completely spoilt. The orders he made were invariably for the benefit of others. They were the 'right thing to do'. He wanted to do the wrong thing for once. With her.

And she knew it. He felt her pulse hammering against his fingers and his body tightened. She'd been bothered by his supposed betrothal. *Jealous?* He knew the feeling.

'What's the video?' he asked, unable to resist his curiosity.

Her blue eyes shimmered. 'You really don't know?'

'I really don't.'

'What sort of security team have you got?'

'A very good one. But I haven't read the report they compiled on you.'

'You weren't interested?'

He couldn't answer that.

Her gaze dropped. 'Please don't look at it.'

His muscles were so tense they ached. Whatever it was clearly mortified her and he carefully considered his words. 'Did someone take advantage of you?'

He wanted to know if someone *hurt* her. Because if that were the case he'd grind their bones. His imagination was going overtime but he didn't want to hurt her more.

She swallowed. 'Not in the way you're thinking.'

He breathed out. 'I'm sorry that happened. I won't look for it.'

She nodded but he had the feeling she didn't quite believe him. Which meant people had made promises to her in the past only to break them. Having one's trust violated hurt, deeply. He knew that too.

Guilt rose. She'd lost her job and he hadn't known because he'd been too angry to bother finding out the truth. He should have looked for her. Instead he'd decided not to purely because he was bothered about how much she'd bothered him. Now he had to move because there was too little time. He wanted her to at least have some fun tonight. And not the horizontal sort.

A 'trip to the zoo'. Her acerbic retort made him

smile. He had a quixotic desire to see her enjoying the celebrations. He pulled out his phone.

'Your Majesty?'

'Send Callie to Amalia's suite in ten minutes.'

'Of course, sir.'

He carried the mandolin case and led Elsie through the back corridors, aware of the curiosity of the palace guards but none dared meet his eyes or ask questions.

Amalia's face lit up the second she saw Elsie.

'It's my fault Elsie left.' Felipe spoke smoothly before Elsie could. 'My security team were invasive and Elsie's employer got the wrong idea. They let her go. That's why she couldn't return to the palace. She had to leave Silvabon the next day.'

The colour was building in Elsie's cheeks. Hadn't she expected him to tell his stepsister the truth?

'That's *terrible*.' Amalia's eyes widened.

'It is,' he agreed. 'I've apologised—profusely—and asked her to join us tonight.'

'You're coming to the boring banquet?' Amalia spun towards Elsie. 'I didn't want to go but if you're coming—'

'Callie's on her way,' Felipe said to Amalia. 'Can you help her find something for Elsie? You have good taste and you know the kind of thing required, right?'

Amalia stood a little taller. 'I think so.'

'Is that okay with you, Elsie?' He finally faced her fully again.

There was a glint in her eyes but she didn't argue. 'Great.'

Felipe left them to it, unable to stand being in Elsie's company any longer. But he was aware that Amalia had suddenly looked livelier than she had in months. She was lonely. He needed to do better for her and once this time-sucking ceremony was over he'd take her to investigate those schools properly.

He walked into his office and five people froze. They were already aware of his instructions and invitation regarding Elsie and it was as if he'd dropped a bomb on them. Maybe he had. Felipe had always done everything expected of him. Today an air of the unexpected infiltrated. He found he quite liked it.

'Everything's in hand, right?' he asked mildly.

His PA glanced around and was the one who stepped forward first. 'Some of the Europeans have asked if you'd like a meeting—'

'Not today.' Felipe didn't let him finish. 'I need to focus on the coronation.' Actually he needed to focus on *regaining* his focus. 'Please assure them that in the coming weeks I'll make time for them and I'll greet everyone tonight at the banquet.'

Everyone stilled again. Yes, that wasn't the answer they'd expected. Ordinarily he'd make a meeting if requested. But trade talks could wait. He had very few personal moments left before the ceremony.

'The passengers who are stuck at the airport,' he said thoughtfully.

'Sir?'

'Is there any way we could give them a tour or something in the morning? So they don't feel imprisoned in that hotel for the full twenty-four hours?' He rolled his shoulders, trying to think of something—anything—but Elsie. 'A bus tour? A walk around the vineyard at the other side of the island? Then back to watch the coronation on the big screen at the airport before they leave?'

His assistant looked hesitant. 'It would be a logistical challenge.'

'But one I know you're capable of pulling off. It would a gesture of goodwill for the inconvenience they're suffering—something to alleviate the impact we've had on their time and liberty.'

'Of course.'

'Your Majesty.' Garcia stepped forward. 'Someone's been in touch about Ms Wynter.'

Felipe paused. He needed to talk to Garcia about what had happened. 'Clear the room.'

Stillness again, then a sudden exodus.

Felipe eyed Garcia. 'Who?'

'One of the passengers on her flight asked airport security.' Major Garcia avoided his gaze and read from the tablet he held in front of him. 'Peter Sainz was seated across the aisle from Ms Wynter in the plane. A financier from Barcelona, he was concerned that she'd disappeared from the terminal.'

So Ms Wynter raised protective instincts in other people? Felipe's own possessiveness tightened. 'You can let him know she's safe and will return for the flight tomorrow.'

Garcia stiffened. 'Will she attend the coronation as well, sir?'

'No.' It was an instant, gut-instinct answer. 'The plane will depart immediately after the ceremony. She'll be at the airport ready to board with the other passengers at that time.' She'd be gone from his life for good then.

Major Garcia didn't step away.

'You have thoughts on that, Major?' Felipe regarded the man who'd been Head of Security for the last twenty years. His grandfather's iron fist. The man who'd spectacularly failed once and who'd worked excessively hard to make up for it ever since.

'Did you ever read my report on Ms Wynter, sir?'

'I wasn't aware I requested a report from you.' He allowed his voice to drop to an icy whisper. 'Major Garcia?'

Garcia's nostrils flared. Yeah. It was time to remember who the King was in the room.

'When Ms Wynter came to the palace I thought it would be prudent to check her background more comprehensively.'

Felipe's anger grew. 'And you did that immediately?'

'Sir.' Garcia nodded.

'You went to the café while she was at the palace and asked her employers about her?'

'Sir.'

'Without my instruction.'

Garcia stiffened. 'It is my remit to protect you and your family from any threats.'

'You didn't trust the work Ortiz had already done?'

'With respect, it wasn't detailed enough.'

Possibly true but beside the point. 'I had told him to hold off on a full check.'

Garcia stood his ground. 'Would you like to see the report, sir?'

'No.'

'But—'

'No.' Felipe straightened. 'I appreciate your concern, Garcia. And I respect that you need to do your job but in this instance you overstepped the mark. Furthermore, you were *not* discreet. The resulting impact on Ms Wynter was unacceptable. It damages the monarchy's reputation that she was dismissed because of palace interference. Can you imagine the media headlines if that were to get out?'

Garcia swallowed.

'The fact it *hasn't* been leaked is a credit to Ms Wynter.'

'But—'

'But nothing. I trust that your team has the entire island at maximum security. You may be assured Ms Wynter is no threat to me, Amalia or any of the dignitaries here for the coronation. Tonight's banquet is a sealed occasion and she will depart the palace tomorrow and the country moments after the coronation, which she will *not* attend. I am confident you will be able to keep her identity and attendance tonight under wraps. Am I clear?'

'Of course, Your Majesty.'

'Thank you. That will be all.'

He didn't want to read the report. He didn't want to watch the video.

What he wanted was so much worse than that.

Elsie was amazed at the efficiency of Felipe's staff. They'd had a selection of dresses delivered in less than an hour—during which a trio of stylists had descended to begin work on her hair and nails. It was only in this brief moment that she and Amalia were actually alone and even then Amalia was burrowing through the rack of dresses.

'I'm sorry you had to leave so suddenly.' Amalia smiled awkwardly at Elsie. 'Felipe shouldn't have done that.'

'I don't think it was necessarily his fault,' Elsie said slowly, realising she'd actually believed him when he'd said he hadn't known his team were going to investigate her.

'We could skip the banquet altogether,' Amalia suggested. 'I could say I have a rash and we could just stay up here and play music.'

Elsie laughed. 'As nice as that idea is, I don't think we can do that.'

'Why not? He won't even notice if I'm not there.'

'I think he would, actually,' Elsie said softly. 'I

know he's very busy but he's concerned for you. I think he doesn't want you to be alone. So…let's go together.'

'Okay, then, what about this one?' Amalia held up a scarlet dress, her eyes sparkling.

'Oh, um. I think that might make me stand out too much.' Honestly, she was terrified.

Amalia looked curious. 'You don't want to stand out?'

'Definitely not.' Elsie laughed. 'I don't really fit in here, Amalia. And I definitely don't think I can wear something like *that*.'

'I don't really fit in here either.' But Amalia suddenly smiled. 'We can not fit in together.'

'Discreetly.' Elsie nodded.

'You want discreet.' Amalia shook her head. 'That's disappointing.'

Elsie didn't just want discreet. She wanted wallpaper—something in which she'd melt into the background. She had no desire to be Cinderella and make everyone stop and stare and wonder who she was. She wanted to enjoy the evening with anonymity.

Just over half an hour later Elsie wriggled her toes. 'It'll be fun. She said. It'll be quick. She said.'

She shot Amalia a look from the chair in which she was being very, very still so the hairdresser and make-up artist and nail technician could all work miracles. 'I'm super glad I am not a princess.'

'Me too.' Amalia chuckled. 'But you have to admit this is a little bit fun.'

Yeah, Elsie hadn't really meant it. Because the secret pleasure of having people wash and comb out her hair, paint her nails and make her feel pretty? It was lovely. She'd apologised a billion times because she hadn't had a trim in for ever, but the hairdresser had brushed aside her murmurings with a smile.

'The dress is perfect,' Amalia added, looking pleased.

Amalia had helped her choose a column dress the deep navy of Silvabon. The fact it was both sleeveless and strapless had been a sticking point, but it was the best of the bunch in terms of subtlety and that was what she wanted. Inoffensive and not eye-catching. Elsie didn't want to breathe in case it slipped. Amalia assured her it wouldn't and the seamstress had supplied her with tape.

'Which shoes?' Amalia danced in front of the five pairs Callie had set out.

'I can't do heels that high,' Elsie shook her head at the stunning black stilettos with the red sole.

'Satin ballet slippers?' Amalia held some up.

'Mmm, not going to make me any taller.'

'What did you want, stilts?' An amused voice came from behind them.

Elsie spun around and Amalia smothered her giggle.

'I've told you before not to sneak up on people,' she said bluntly. 'Especially when they're still getting *dressed*.'

'You look dressed to me.' His gaze dropped down her body.

Fiery awareness flickered across her skin as he took in her appearance, but she hadn't exactly rendered him speechless. Whereas now *she'd* taken a second to see him? She almost swallowed her tongue.

He was wearing a tuxedo with a navy sash that had gold trim and an insignia. Not full royal regalia but enough to remind all who he was. The star of the show. Her pulse skipped infuriatingly. Her reaction in secret places? Mortifying.

'Are you wearing that bathrobe tonight, Amalia?' Felipe asked idly.

'Two minutes.' Amalia dashed to her dressing room.

Without another word, the assistants cleared the room.

Elsie stared as the door closed behind them and then turned to look at him. 'Does it take them long to master the mind-reading thing?'

He chuckled. 'You didn't see my signal.'

'You literally just lift your little finger? Is that so you don't tire your voice?'

He ignored her and scooped up a pair of shoes. 'These would be good.'

She ground her teeth, not wanting to give him the points for picking the best pair. Mid-level heel but with pretty straps. 'You're not putting them on me.'

'So that's a yes?' He smiled.

She awkwardly took the shoes from his hand. 'Thank you, fairy god—'

'I will silence you with my little finger, Elsie,' he said huskily. 'Or better yet, make you scream.'

She froze at the shockingly sexually tinged threat. Then bent to hide the scorching blush on her skin. *With just his little finger?*

'I'm pleased,' he murmured as she strapped on the shoes. 'Generally you manage to ignore most things I suggest.'

'Was it a *suggestion*?' she echoed. 'I thought it was another of your orders. You being the King and all.'

He chuckled. 'As a guest of Silvabon you are required to abide by the laws of the country. Including the orders of the King. But tonight I waive that requirement—just for lucky little you, you understand.'

'Wow.' She straightened.

He regarded her, suddenly serious. 'I vow, I won't order you to do anything. Not tonight. I'm not a king. For you, Elsie, I'll be just a man.'

She couldn't move. His words? The way he was gazing at her?

She was suddenly so self-conscious.

'Amalia said this dress would be suitable,' she stammered.

Why was she seeking his approval? It didn't matter what he thought. But her mouth was dry and that moment kept flashing in her mind—when he'd told her to leave, when it had looked as if that was the *last* thing he'd wanted her to do, when he'd almost kissed her. The look in his eyes now matched that. As if a storm were raging—a war between want and denial.

'You look immaculate.'

'Are you sure about this?' she asked.

'People will be informed that you're here as a guest of Amalia's.'

'Like her music tutor?' She nodded. 'That could definitely work.'

'Music tutor it is.'

'They won't know my full name, will they? And I won't be seated near you, will I?'

A half-smile quirked his lips. 'This inferiority complex you've got going...we're equal, are we not? I thought I'd just made that clear.'

'No. We're not. You know we're not.'

Before he could reply Amalia appeared. But there was a look in his eye that promised they'd continue the conversation later. But that wasn't happening. It couldn't.

'You look stunning, Amalia,' he said.

'I'm only doing this for her,' Elsie whispered as they followed Amalia along the corridor.

'You can think that if it makes you feel better.'

CHAPTER EIGHT

Friday, 7.03 p.m.

ELSIE'S NERVES TIGHTENED, but Felipe didn't take her straight to the ballroom. Instead they stopped at a small chamber not far from Amalia's suite. A selection of velvet boxes had been set out on the table.

'I know you appreciate and enjoy jewellery.' He gestured for Amalia to step forward. 'You may choose something to wear tonight.'

Amalia's eyes rounded. 'Are you sure?'

'Of course,' he said. 'Take your time. You can try them all.'

The waiting maid showed Amalia earrings, necklaces, jewelled hair combs, even a couple of miniature tiaras. After a moment Felipe walked over to where Elsie was quietly marvelling.

'Your skin is also bare.' He pulled something from his pocket. 'Perhaps you would like to wear this?'

Elsie's skin rippled with goosebumps as he held it for her to inspect. A narrow rope of glistening diamonds set in gold. It sparkled brilliantly, making her think of an unbreakable chain that would undeniably *tie* her to him. She stared into his eyes for a smouldering moment, shocked by her thoughts...at the temptation at the thought of being so *linked* to him.

'It's a bracelet,' he explained slowly as if she'd suddenly become brainless.

Which apparently she had because now a vision rose—of herself clad in nothing but this diamond chain on her wrist and with Felipe bracing above her, the wickedest of smiles on his face. A ball of heat exploded low in her belly.

'No.' She shook her head, clearing the shocking image. 'No.'

'It's just a bracelet. Just for tonight.'

'What happened to "my body my rules"? Adornment?' she asked, desperate to escape her own overactive imagination. 'You said you weren't my fairy godmother, but you want to dress me up to fit in with your world.'

'It's not that. You'll never fit into my world.'

The truth stung.

He gripped her wrist and stopped her from stepping away. 'That's a good thing, Elsie.'

'If it's good, then don't ask me to pretend to be someone I'm not.'

'Can you not be someone who wears pretty things? Or expensive things? Do you think you're not worthy in some way?'

His perception angered her. She needed to stop him. To shock him. And there was nothing more shocking than the truth. As he'd just demonstrated. 'My father is in prison.'

He stilled. 'Your father is not you.'

She felt the prickle of tears and blinked rapidly,

resisting the overwhelming emotion. It seemed more truth might be required. Things she never spoke of. She needed to push him away from her. 'My brother was in prison too.'

'But *you're* not.' He hesitated. 'Have you ever been?'

She slowly shook her head.

His eyes were very deep and dark and he regarded her steadily. 'And your mother's gone. I'm sorry, Elsie.'

It hadn't worked. He hadn't withdrawn. Now he actually stepped closer, lifting the bracelet in his hand.

'Please, Felipe.' She shook her head again. He could tempt her into wearing it. Part of her desperately wanted to—to be accepted, to pretend for just a little while. Another part wanted to snatch it from his hand and *never* give it back. 'It's not mine. It's not something I earned and I paid for. It's not appropriate.'

'It's only to borrow, not keep,' he argued. 'Amalia told me you didn't want to stand out. Unadorned you will. I imagine Sofia will be wearing so many kilos of jewels she'll barely be able to stand beneath the weight of them.'

Startled, a horrible hot sensation rolled through her stomach. 'She's going to be here tonight?'

'Are you jealous of my ex?'

Her gaze flew back to him. 'Is that what she is?'

'Not really.' His intensity sharpened and his voice dropped. 'We didn't sleep together.'

Embarrassment burned, yet relief swamped her. 'You didn't need to tell me that.'

'No?'

'You wouldn't have slept with her until you were married.'

He looked at her quizzically, then began to laugh. 'Virgin princesses are the stuff of fairy tales, Elsie.'

She burned worse now. 'You've slept with other princesses?'

He puffed out a breath. 'None of my former lovers will be present tonight.'

'This information is too personal to be relevant to me,' she gritted.

He merely laughed harder—but the warmth in his gaze?

'You sure you want to trust me with this?' She tried to shoot him down.

'You've not told anyone about your time in the palace all those months ago and you could have. You wouldn't expose Amalia. You wouldn't hurt me either.'

'Not even if someone paid me pots of money?'

'You could have sold your story weeks ago and you didn't. Your integrity matters too much to you.'

Just like that he stole her breath for good.

'I trust you, Elsie. I wouldn't invite you to wear this if I didn't.'

Tears prickled. That he trusted her *mattered* intensely and it meant so very much. But it suddenly saddened her. He was one of the few people to believe in her and he was so far from her reach. It was the most bittersweet feeling.

'Thank you for the offer. I'm honoured,' she said simply. 'But no. The dress is enough. I'm her music tutor,' she said. 'No one expects me to be dripping with diamonds.'

He gazed into her eyes solemnly. 'As you wish.' He put the fistful of jewels back into his pocket and called to Amalia. 'Are you ready?'

The girl turned. She'd chosen a pretty pearl necklet that was just gorgeous.

'Silvabon pearls.' Felipe nodded. 'Nice choice, Amalia. Several in that piece were found off one of the smaller islands many years ago.'

Amalia fingered the necklet gently. 'Is it true you used to go diving for them?'

Felipe's eyebrows lifted. 'You heard about that?'

'Carlos said that one time you were free diving and you went under for so long the bodyguards all jumped in fully clothed to rescue you. But then you surfaced and you laughed so hard. Carlos said you'd found an amazing pearl.'

Felipe blinked. 'He told you that story?'

'He talked about you all the time,' Amalia said. 'He said you found lots.'

There was a flash on Felipe's face that made Elsie instinctively step closer to him.

But Amalia hadn't noticed. 'He said the old King banned you from diving again after that.'

There was a beat before Felipe answered. Where Elsie realised he'd taken a moment to count himself down. He glanced at her and his shoulders squared because, yes, she'd seen.

'He might've made a *suggestion* along those lines.' Felipe shot her one of those devastating stares.

'But you dived anyway,' Elsie surmised wryly, understanding he needed a moment of levity. 'And there we all thought you *kept* your promises…'

'I didn't promise him I wouldn't dive.' Felipe winked. 'He suggested that I refrained from it. I chose not to listen.'

'Carlos said you have more courage than anyone.' Amalia nodded, oblivious to the charged undercurrent that returned at her words. 'Do you still find them?'

This time Felipe didn't reply.

'Felipe?' Elsie said softly.

'I haven't had much time to dive there recently.' He didn't look at either of them.

'I wish I could try,' Amalia said wistfully. 'But I can't swim well.'

Felipe cleared his throat. 'We all have different strengths. I can't play the piano at all.'

Amalia touched the necklet again and suddenly lifted her chin. 'I'll teach you a tune if you teach me to dive.'

For another silent moment both step-siblings

stood frozen. Elsie desperately sought Felipe's gaze, and as he glanced towards her she stared at him meaningfully.

Say yes to her. Please.

That muscle in his jaw flicked. 'Okay.' He nodded briskly at Amalia. 'Sure. Later in summer when your leg is stronger.'

Elsie's heart pounded. She was stupidly relieved because the two of them could be closer and that would be good for them both.

'Good motivation to do your physio exercises.' She smiled at Amalia. 'You look so pretty. The pearls are perfect.'

Felipe walked with them through the labyrinthine corridors towards the reception room. Just as they arrived, he dropped husky words in her ear. 'By the way, did you really think you wouldn't stand out in that dress?'

She smiled, his tease soothing her nerves and assuring her he'd recovered from that moment. Of course he had. He was a king and had consummate control of everything. 'I was hoping to blend in with the banners.'

He shook his head and peeled away from them.

'Felipe said we don't have to do the greeting line, we go in another entrance,' Amalia said. 'I don't know how he remembers everyone's names. There are hundreds of them.'

Elsie watched him, trying to be surreptitious and totally failing. It didn't matter; no one was paying attention to her. He stood at the opposite end of the banquet hall, ready to greet his guests, tall and strong and obviously comfortable. But he was also isolated. Even with courtiers and government ministers waiting with him, he was set apart. It wasn't just that air of command, that he was full-fleshed authority to the bone, the one from whom all sought approval. Everyone in this vast room ached to impress him yet there was no one at his side. No partner. No family. Not even his mother. He was starkly alone. And that, she realised, was how he wanted it.

He'd never wanted to marry that princess. He'd not wanted Amalia to suffer through the boredom of the reception line. He saw this all as solely *his* duty—as he stood beneath the portrait of his steely-eyed grandfather. Given any image of his father had been scrubbed long ago, only Felipe remained now. It was down to him. And that was how he'd keep it.

As she studied him, he turned. Unerringly his gaze met hers. There was a moment when she felt the intensity as if he were standing but a breath from her. A moment later liveried guards swung the wide oak door open and the procession of guests began. In minutes there were several princesses in the room. Their dresses were sleek and glamorous. She and Amalia amused themselves in admiring them, then Elsie had to focus on enjoying the musicians' skill because she was inordinately jealous of the women talking to Felipe. She'd recognised the princess he wasn't marrying. She was wearing a golden dress and looked like a goddess.

'I want to learn the drums,' Amalia said.

Yeah, Elsie had the urge to bash loud things with heavy sticks this second.

More princes. Kings. Prime ministers. Presidents. Security was obvious and tight. Elsie understood why the skies had been closed. There was a detail on Amalia. She saw the men from the café watching at a discreet distance.

Like every guest there, she was hyper aware of where Felipe was. Who he was talking to. He was an absolute professional—greeting every guest by name, circulating, allowing everyone moments of his attention. The thing they all craved most.

The air of excitement and celebration was palpable. The banquet hall glittered with polished silver and chandeliers. The food was sublime but Elsie found she couldn't eat much. She smiled politely as nearby guests talked to Amalia about places to visit in Europe. She considered them all like customers, inquiring politely, admiring something. Her introduction as Amalia's music assistant was accepted without question. After the feast they headed to the ballroom. She and Amalia were left more to themselves.

Felipe needed to stop staring at her, but *not* staring at her felt even more obvious. He couldn't find the balance. It was stupid and in overthinking it he found his gaze drifting towards her again. With nothing around her neck, no jewel to distract the eye, there was no escaping the beauty of her smooth skin, the desperately tempting line of her collar-bones. He couldn't get enough of the stunning scope of her bare skin. He wanted to see more—everything that lay beneath that demure neckline of the dress. Her hair was highlighted and gleaming like a halo. She didn't need a tiara for people to take notice of her.

At her side Amalia was laughing, while Elsie was more circumspect. But her glacial blue eyes burned like the hottest flames whenever her gaze clashed with his.

Why had he wanted to adorn her? Why when she couldn't sparkle any more than she currently did? The bracelet was still in his pocket. He'd imagined it sparkling on her wrist as she played her mandolin. A hint of perspiration popped at the thought of her curled on his bed wearing nothing but those diamonds, waiting for him to pet her. What was with the dominant fantasies? He'd never explored that kind of play before. But he ached for her complete submission to him. Not as a king, but as a man. As the lover to whom she would allow absolute access—to every inch of her skin, to those secrets in her soul. He wanted complete *possession*. And equally he ached to fall to his knees before her and feel the honour of her touch, her caress.

The power she could wield over him was startling

in its intensity and the dominance in his thinking. He could never allow lust to bring him—and the monarchy—to its knees.

She *was* a threat. He hadn't known that members of her family were in prison. He ought to know why already. But he'd ignored Garcia's warnings. Hell, he was turning into his father—turning his back on duty to indulge in lust. And the worst thing was he didn't care. But he did feel a qualm of guilt for *her*. She didn't want exposure. She wasn't part of this world. She'd never faced paparazzi, never should.

It was too late to banish her from the palace again, but she would leave tomorrow and he would never see her again. She would be safe.

Right this second he wanted to turn back the clock and return to medieval times when a king had concubines and kept chosen mistresses in court, ready for his attention. He wanted to send everyone packing with a finger snap. He wanted *all* the freedoms, *all* the time and he wanted it *all* with her.

He tried to maintain polite conversation. Tried to ensure that he worked his way around all the dignitaries so he didn't unintentionally offend anyone. Honestly, the greeting line had been endless, even for a royal of his experience...

Now Elsie glanced over. He had to stay very still so he didn't give away his unguarded rushing response. He was unwilling, unable to release her gaze... Until the prime minister spoke to him and directed him to another dignitary who'd been waiting. No, he couldn't speak to her yet. He'd not allow himself near until he'd controlled his desire to touch her.

People danced in the ballroom. He didn't. He never did—never favoured anyone in public at any rate. A few more minutes passed and he'd lost sight of them.

'Where are they?' He frowned at Ortiz. 'Why aren't you with them?'

'They're secure within the private wing, Your Majesty.' Ortiz replied. 'They left about twenty minutes ago.'

Yeah, he knew exactly how many minutes it was since he'd been able to see her. She'd left the banquet before the King gave his consent? No one did that. Amalia was only allowed given her age. Except he'd given Elsie a reprieve tonight, hadn't he? He was not her king. But had she really thought she could leave him again without saying goodbye?

Not this time.

CHAPTER NINE

Friday, 11.27 p.m.

ELSIE WALKED DOWN the long corridor, hoping it would lead to the guest wing. She should've asked Amalia's maid to show her but hadn't wanted to be a pain. It was so quiet this far from the ballroom she felt as if she were the only person in some magical realm.

'You didn't even make it to midnight before running away.' A tall shadow stepped from a corner.

'Felipe?' Her jump-scare switched to jump-sizzle as he moved closer until he was right in front of her.

She could hardly look at him in that sharp suit with the glimmer of stubble on his sculpted jaw and the smouldering ferocity in his eyes.

'Amalia is over it,' Elsie nervously explained. 'She's just gone to bed.'

'I'm over it too,' he muttered.

Elsie couldn't think about *him* going to bed. 'What about your guests?'

'I've talked with all of them.' His stormy gaze pierced her. 'Except you.'

'I'm not your guest, though. I'm—'

'Here under sufferance?' he interjected huskily.

'Here for Amalia,' she corrected softly.

'No, you're not.'

Her pulse flicked into double time. Amalia had been one reason he'd demanded her presence tonight. But there was another—stronger one.

Take a breath.

It was impossible. Hot and tense, she needed to get away from him.

'I'm going to my room.' Her voice wobbled worse than an opera diva's.

'Is it satisfactory?'

She hadn't actually seen it yet. She'd got ready in Amalia's room, where they'd provided literally everything for her. Dress, shoes...*panties*. But before she could answer him, he frowned heavily.

'It's in the guest wing,' he growled.

'Speaking of guests,' she answered awkwardly. 'You really should get back to them.'

'I don't want to.'

She couldn't help a smile. 'You do sullen far better than your teenage stepsister.'

'I'm not sure it's wise to provoke me right now, Elsie.'

Her mouth dried.

'I've let it be known I've retired to reflect before tomorrow,' he said.

Tomorrow was too close already. Time was ticking—trickling away.

'To reflect?' She reached for a smile but failed.

At midday tomorrow he would be the sole focus of millions of people. She couldn't imagine the pressure that came with that level of scrutiny.

He shrugged. 'The banquet ends at midnight anyway, so the guests may be fully rested before the coronation.'

'But you can't miss the fireworks.'

A wicked smile glimmered in his eyes as he leaned too close and whispered, 'I don't intend to.'

Adrenalin raced, setting off a raucous, wicked temptation.

'What about you?' he added. 'You're all dressed up and it's not even midnight and you're running away.'

She wasn't—she was fixed to the spot when she should be running through the castle—running from *him*. But she couldn't pull herself free of his mesmerising presence.

'You didn't dance.' His eyes were full of regret and his voice was so quiet she was unsure he even meant her to hear. 'I wanted to dance with you. But I couldn't.'

'Couldn't or wouldn't?'

'They'd eat you alive. I can't let that happen.'

A last barrier melted inside her. 'You're trying to protect me?' Was that why he'd kept at such a disappointing distance all evening? It wasn't that he'd forgotten about her.

'Their pursuit would be relentless.'

He was so close her mind spun and she lost control. That dangerous part of her spilled free. 'What about your pursuit?' she asked huskily. 'Would that be relentless?'

His eyes widened. He stood still before her but his fingers touched hers. So lightly. So carefully. 'Are you flirting with me? Finally?'

Only a very little. 'You don't need to protect me from anyone,' she said. 'I'm leaving tomorrow and I'm not coming back.'

His fingers interlinked with hers—the softest, most fragile of connections. Electricity surged—striking a chord deep within her.

'Dance with me.' There was a thread of steel in his voice now.

'Here? We can't even hear the music.'

'You're musical. Hum something.'

'Any other orders?' she asked with an arch of her brows.

'So many, I'm struggling to hold them all back.'

She couldn't suppress the shiver of sensual intrigue. 'Is that so?'

His jaw locked. 'Temptress.'

Was she? 'I thought I was Cinderella. But I'm not—that's you.'

Genuine surprise flickered on his face, then amusement. *'Me?'*

'You're trapped in a palace, doing all the work—cleaning up the messes your family left. You ensure everyone has everything they need…'

'Then don't say no. Dance with me,' he said simply. 'Just once.'

It felt so much more than a mere invitation to dance.

'Because you ask so nicely?' she teased.

'Please.' He stepped back and held his hand out to her.

It was such an old-fashioned formal gesture it made her smile. She put her hand in his, half expecting—hoping—he'd haul her to him, but he kept a courteous distance. His posture was ballroom-dancer perfect. She rested her hand lightly on his shoulder. She could feel the rigidity of his muscles. There was no softening into an embrace. He stared into her eyes, watching, waiting.

There was always that pause, the beat before the music began when one was supposed to take a breath. But Elsie couldn't breathe at all.

'Elsie?' He nodded, a gorgeous encouragement. 'Make some music.'

She barely hummed and only for long enough to establish the rhythm. He picked it up and led her into a waltz—intimate yet constrained.

They were in a bubble of their own. The atmosphere thickened, heated. Touching him? Finally feeling the breadth of his shoulders, the leashed strength in his achingly near body, unlocked something that had long been caged. Something she hadn't wanted to admit existed, let alone allow out. It was a part of her she'd wanted to hide. *Greed.*

She couldn't hum anything any more, but the rhythm between them pulsed regardless and they slowly danced down the darkening corridor. As they passed each low burning light, she caught the gleam in his eyes—the considering look, the curve of his lips.

'Where are you taking me?' She was breathless—as if they'd been dancing a foxtrot, not a carefully controlled waltz.

'Somewhere secret.'

He released her to open a door. A flick made lights illuminate the room.

She paused and took in the glittering space. 'You have a whole other ballroom?'

It was smaller than the one downstairs currently filled with visiting dignitaries from nations around the world, but equally stunning—if not more. This one was gold—figurines and frescoes—cherubs and smiling nymphs all in suggestive scenes.

'This is a salon for private performances,' he explained.

'*Private* performances?' She shot him a look. 'What sort of performances?'

'Not the sort you're thinking. At least, not in the last decade or two. Maybe last century it was for—'

'Orgies?'

'Perhaps my forefathers enjoyed personal dances here.' He held out his hand, inviting her to dance again, only this time in this gorgeous small ballroom.

So easily she slid back into temptation—where all that mattered was his touch, his movement, his nearness, his damned breath. Could she let his seduction happen so easily?

'I think Amalia enjoyed tonight,' she muttered, desperately trying to distract herself for just a second.

His shoulder tightened. 'It'll be better for her at boarding school.'

'Do you think?' Elsie's heart ached. 'Is it not a fairy tale to be rescued by a brother who's a king—taken to an idyllic island in the middle of the Mediterranean? To live in a palace and not have to worry?'

'It's no fairy tale.' His expression twisted. 'She lacks friends her own age and normal freedoms.'

Yeah, Elsie had been aware of the girl's isolation when she'd first met her at the café. 'You still don't want her to stay here?'

'The press were beyond cruel to Amalia's mother and to my own. I want to protect Amalia from that future. The only reason she's not already at boarding school is because she needed time to recover, not just from her own injuries, but from the loss of her parents.'

Had Felipe recovered? It was his father who'd died too. In fact, Elsie realised, Felipe had lost his father twice—years ago when he'd abdicated, then again when he'd died in the accident. How had he adjusted to that? And to his mother vowing never to return to the palace?

Elsie had been older than him when she'd lost her mother. And then she'd been ostracised by everyone. People she'd considered close hadn't believed in her innocence. It had been so easy for them to think the worst, so easy for them to cast her out alone. Alone sucked. Alone was hard. Elsie didn't want either Amalia or Felipe to be alone and they didn't need to be. They could have each other. Amalia had reached out already tonight when she'd asked about the pearls. If Felipe allowed it...

'But she's okay here, Felipe,' she said nervously.

'Tonight she smiled for the first time in weeks. Thank you for that.'

'It *wasn't* me.' It had been *him*.

His gaze intensified. 'You don't think?'

In the distance a clock chimed. By unspoken agreement they stilled, counting the beats. Twelve. Midnight. As the last chime resonated through the room, there was a sudden volley of bangs like gunfire. She jumped in fright. Only this time he had hold of her. And this time he pulled her closer.

'Fireworks,' he murmured.

The explosions echoed even through the thick walls. But Elsie was safe, pressed against his solid, hot body—in an embrace that was so secure she shivered.

Cinderella was all wrong. The magic didn't *end* at midnight, it was only then that it *began*. Secret, wonderful things could only happen under cover of darkness when everyone else was asleep. When no one would see. Now was *her* time.

'The next time that clock strikes twelve your time will be up. You'll be crowned.' She smiled at him a little sadly. 'My poor Cinder-fella, stuck in a life of duty.'

'Cinder-fella?' He rolled his eyes.

She'd giggle if she didn't actually feel sorry for him.

'The coronation is a formality, Elsie. It's not as bad as you think. Fundamentally, nothing will change.'

No? But she saw resignation smothering restlessness in his eyes. Cemented, regimented, he was bracing for a constrained future.

'A very public formality,' she said.

His expression grew stormy. He didn't want her pity. Just as she didn't want his. They didn't have the time to waste on it.

'Be careful, I'll take advantage of your compassion.' He backed her into a corner. 'And I'll ask for things you shouldn't give me.'

'Such as?' she breathed.

'Everything.' He cupped her jaw—holding her in place. With her lips upturned to his, this was a prelude to a kiss. 'Say no to me.'

His breath skimmed over her mouth, making her shiver, but she stayed silent.

'Say *no* to me,' he repeated—urgent and imperious. But his eyes asked another question altogether.

She still didn't answer. He was the merest breath from her now.

'Say no, damn it.' His tone splintered.

So did her temper. Why should she make it easy

for him? Why should *she* have to bear the burden of doing the right thing? She'd done that before and it had hurt her badly. What was the point in trying to be good? She'd still lost—everything. And this once she wanted something for herself.

She lifted her chin as anger and desire overwhelmed her. *'No.'*

His mouth parted and he froze, but before he could snap away from her she hooked her arm around his neck and held him close. His eyes were blown—as black as midnight, as endless, as aching.

'Not what you wanted to hear after all?' she jeered, but her voice shook. So did her body. She arched towards him like a tulip leaning towards the sun. Craving. Yielding. His mere nearness unleashed the part of her that wanted to take all and damn the consequences. The greedy, selfish, reckless part and she didn't care any more. Her energy was bursting at her seams. She wanted him to release it. She didn't want him to be anything but honest and raw. Now.

'What do you *really* want?' she asked, angry and aching. 'Tell me the truth.' It was an order of her own.

His hands dropped to her waist. He closed the gap completely and the weight of him pressed the breath from her body.

'You. Bed. Mine,' he snarled. *'Mine.'*

'Yours.' She murmured her assent and melted.

There was nowhere she could go. Nowhere else she'd rather be.

He pressed her harder against the wall and held her gaze before nipping her lower lip—so lightly, so gently, so quick, she gasped. It was intimate. Dominant. Playful. And a promise. In a blink he was back with the gentlest of kisses. Elsie shuddered—aching, accepting, surrendering it all.

This man had everything. He stood at the apex of the world, ruler of an entire country, an island of riches and beauty. He was a man who apparently had everything. Yet he had so very little for *himself*. And he wanted her.

Sensations exploded—taste and scent and touch. Felipe was everywhere and everything—seeking her very soul with a sublime kiss. His tongue stroked and his lips pressed and it was so heady she was lost. Any last space between them was gone as they sealed together. His hardness pressed against her belly and she pressed back. She gave but he wanted more and the more she gave, the more he wanted. But it was the same for her. Wedged between him and the wall was the best. Breathless, crushed. Every cell sang. It was a line call between laughter and tears as she unashamedly rubbed against him with a mewl of pure agony, pure delight.

At that he tore free and stared into her eyes. The torture in his made her freeze.

'Elsie, I don't...' He huffed a breath. 'I don't want...'

He'd stopped. He *wanted* to stop. He was conflicted about this, which meant there was a problem. *She* was the problem.

Heat churned into anger—the only acceptable release for it because she couldn't let him see how much she hurt. How could he stop so easily? Why wasn't he as crazed with lust as she was? The one time she'd given into the urge to *take* what she wanted—to be greedy and selfish like her family—she'd been denied. She couldn't win whichever way she tried.

'Aren't you going to ask what I want? Are you making this decision without asking me?' she asked fiercely.

Why had he offered something she wanted so much only to snatch it away from her at the last second? Did he not want it as much as her after all?

Something flickered in his gaze. 'I'm trying to do the right thing.'

But how was this wrong? Here—just here, just now—was the right thing, wasn't it? That part of her that didn't care was released. The greedy, naughty part she'd tried to suppress for years. 'Stop trying to do the right thing and do what you *want* for once in your life,' she snapped.

'And damn the consequences?'

'What consequences? Why will there be any? Nothing bad's going to happen because we both know…' She shook her head in frustration. 'This is it. This is the *one* time we can do what *feels* right, not what we *think* is right. Not what we should do. We have minutes, Felipe. Only minutes.'

This was the one time they had. The *only* time she'd ever *wanted* to. No one would know. No one would judge. Here in his palace they had the safest, most secure, most secret, most solitary of chances.

'Elsie.' A tic in his jaw flicked.

'Why would it be *bad*?' She was unable to stifle her stark honesty, the avaricious need within over-ruling her usual caution. 'You're not a king to me, Felipe. You're just a man I want.'

It would be a brief crossover in lives that were so very different. But he stared at her—still locked against her. As slow seconds ticked by, shame slithered in.

What was she doing? Basically begging the guy to take her to bed? He clearly didn't want to. She was making a fool of herself. She felt ripped open and *unwanted*.

'Forget it.' Overwhelmed, she pushed hard against his chest.

He stepped back.

And she *was* such a fool. She ducked out from him. 'I'm going to my room.'

Three paces towards the door she realised she had no idea how to find the wretched thing. She stopped. 'I'm afraid you need to show me the way.'

She didn't want to look at him but her eyes wouldn't obey her brain. He was standing where she'd left him. Still and frowning at her. And so handsome she wanted to throw something at him. He'd made her want him, so quickly, so easily, so completely. He was her impossible.

'The way?' he echoed.

'I haven't even been to the guest wing.' She put her hands on her hips in a fake gesture of confidence and glared at him. 'You know this place is a rabbit warren. Full of secret corridors that all look the same and lead to…' It was beyond embarrassing now and she growled at him. 'Could you just flick your fingers and have one of your staff magically appear?'

He finally moved. 'I'll show you.'

'*You* don't have to.'

He walked over to where she stood, ignoring her deliberately defiant pose to step in too close and press his hand against her mouth. The gentlest laughter gleamed in his eyes. 'Who's the sulky one now?'

CHAPTER TEN

Saturday, 12.24 a.m.

FELIPE DIDN'T LEAD her back down the corridor but took her deeper into the medieval part of the palace that had once been an impregnable stone fortress. It still was. As the path narrowed he battled his conscience. He wanted her. But that there would be no consequences?

'Is this a short cut?'

Her impatience and defiance made him want to kiss her—to soothe the hurt he knew he'd inflicted. But he couldn't. Yet. 'No.'

He'd tried to resist. But touching her was all he could think about. Dancing had made it worse. He'd asked her to say no, fearing that if she said yes, he wouldn't cope. He hadn't. That kiss had destroyed him. He'd almost taken her hard, against the wall, all control gone. He'd had to slam on the brakes because he was a damned runaway train and he had to make sure she was on board with him. But he'd phrased it poorly. She'd thought he was pulling back. Another miscommunication. When she'd first blown, he'd been awed by her spirit—her fight for him. But her hurt had turned inward, he'd seen the snap in her eyes. He knew she'd felt unworthy and unwanted, which was the absolute opposite of his intention and his truth. She'd stopped mid-fight as if she'd suddenly remembered she had no right to ask for anything. That *wasn't* the surrender he wanted. Giving up? No. She had every right to ask for what she wanted. He wanted to hear it, wanted to enact her demands... His own desire shocked him.

Surely the intensity was a reaction to the relentless preparation and coronation pressures. He just needed a release valve. And they'd had this physical attraction from first sight.

Two silent minutes later she stopped, forcing him to turn and face her.

'Where are you taking me? The dungeon?'

Heat blasted, short-circuiting his brain, and he stepped back into her space. 'Why do I get the feeling you'd like that, Elsie?'

Her eyes widened. *Oh, she would.* With that one flash of desire she damned any lingering good intentions to hell. There was no way he wasn't having her tonight. For all her flightiness, her flashes of temper at his demanding nature, she also craved the dominance he offered. And it worked both ways— the fact was they were imprisoned together by desire. He watched her lift her chin in that show of strength. But they were in thrall to each other. He ached for her submission every bit as much as he ached for her to take him in hand and school him. Released from hesitation and doubt, he knew she'd give him both.

'I'm taking you to my room,' he informed her

bluntly. 'Once there, I'm going to kiss you. Only this time I'll not stop until you ask me to.'

Her eyes glazed. A haze of heated colour washed over every inch of her skin that was visible. 'Promise?'

The husky command almost felled him. He wanted nothing more than to satisfy her. 'I promise.'

He took her hand and led her for another minute along the winding corridor—deliberately taking this route to avoid any courtiers. There was an inevitability about this. He pressed his palm to the security system and opened the door. He released her hand, watching with amusement for her reaction as she stepped into the suite. The sight of Elsie trying to conceal her very obvious emotions brought him immense pleasure. She couldn't, of course; he could see the response in her expressive eyes. She didn't try to hide usually, but this time—was she trying to be polite? Aiming to spare his feelings?

'This is your bedroom?' She turned on the spot, taking it all in until her gaze eventually settled on the large bed. 'Did you decorate it yourself?'

'No,' he replied softly. 'It's been like this for the last century or so.'

She wrinkled her nose. 'Those curtains are over a hundred years old?'

'They've been refurbished, but the decor is as it was originally designed by my many greats grandmother.'

'Was she a performer?' She shot him a look, her

smile bubbling when she saw his amusement. 'Honestly, that's like a proscenium arch at the back of the bed. And what's with all the curtains?'

He leaned back against the door and laughed. Elsie's expression was everything. He studied the surroundings—trying to imagine seeing it for the first time. The room was dressed in navy, black, gold—the colours of Silvabon. Twin candelabras stood either side of the massive bed, making the ornately carved, gilded headboard gleam. Heavy velvet curtains in midnight blue hung behind in gold-fringed swathes. Layers upon layers of the things. Another large crystal chandelier was suspended above them while beneath their feet was thick, intricately woven carpet.

'Has it always been your bedroom?' Elsie murmured.

'It was the most convenient room to take when Grandfather became unwell.'

Right now only the candelabras were lit—with warm bulbs; candles had been phased out a half-century ago. But the effect was undeniably theatrical and lush. For the first time he truly appreciated it because Elsie, dressed in that navy column dress that hugged her curves, fitted perfectly in the centre of the vast, darkened space—like a pearl nestled in an iridescent shell. He wanted to keep her here. Her head was tilted back, exposing the luscious pale skin of her neck as she studied the balcony that ran around the top third of the room.

'Is that for the audience?' she asked. 'Did the royal couple have to…have to do it in front of people to make sure the pregnancy was legitimate or something?'

He watched the colour building in her cheeks. There was a hint of shyness in her stumble over the words, a bigger hint of sensuality in her response to the thought.

'You think they were exhibitionists?' He glanced at the curved wooden staircase that led up to that small mezzanine walkway. 'I've never thought about it. I've never brought a lover back to this room.'

He didn't know why that admission had felt so imperative. No one but his valet came in here. He didn't pay much attention to the room—it was as it had always been. But now as he took in the carved elements of the bed and the balcony, infinite tempting possibilities stirred in his mind.

'You haven't?' Her pale eyes widened. 'Why now?'

It took him a moment to parse the reasons that were bound so tightly with the bare drive of desire. 'It's the safest place we can be together tonight. The room assigned to you is on a relatively busy wing. There's the danger we'd be seen there.'

'And we can't possibly be seen.'

'That's in your best interests.'

'Very concerned for my best interests, aren't you?'

Touched by the wistful vulnerability in her soft

mouth and shy eyes, he pushed away from the door and strolled towards her—immediately gratified by the sensual wariness that smouldered more every step he took.

'I'm very concerned for you, full stop,' he said honestly. 'But I'm willing to do whatever you want me to.'

Rebellion tightened his muscles. His natural instincts were at war. He conceded power to no one, but for Elsie tonight he'd give it in order to take it. One and the same. Everything they both wanted.

'Even if it's *wrong*?'

'I'm yours, Elsie.' He reminded himself of the boundaries to ease his tension. 'Yours until dawn.'

Her eyes sparked with a gleam of something he wasn't sure he could handle.

'Where do you usually take your lovers if not here?' she asked, the colour in her cheeks betraying her. 'You do have lovers, right?'

'Not often.'

'No?' Her eyes glittered.

He chuckled. 'Does that worry you?'

She shook her head and her gaze dropped. 'I hope I'll…'

He clamped his jaw as a hot shaft of possessiveness flooded him. She brushed a stray lock of hair from her face and he saw the tremble in her fingers.

'Tonight is it. All there'll ever be,' he said.

Not because she wasn't worthy. But because he refused to have her endure everything else that came with him. Lovers of princes and kings weren't treated well by the rest of the world, even in this supposedly modern and permissive age. This was a symbolic last moment of freedom. Of choice. Because she wasn't a choice he could make after tomorrow. And that was for her benefit, not his. Tomorrow she'd be gone for good.

'Are you taking a vow of celibacy tomorrow too?' she asked.

He didn't know how it was going to work. An occasional discreet lover here and there. He hadn't considered it until now and, honestly, he didn't care. As long as he had her. Tonight. Now.

She ran her tongue along her lips. 'I think you should stop wasting time...'

For all the bravado she was emotional, maybe even a little nervous. He was going to take care with her. Gentle, savage care. He'd wanted her the moment he'd seen her and she was so close to being his.

Who knew desire could be so total and destructive—tearing reason and rational thought into confetti and scattering it on a storm of lust? But this wasn't just sexual desire. He was drawn to her strength and vulnerability, her humour and earnestness, sassiness and sweetness. He knew her past hindered her and he almost didn't want to know why. It didn't matter what it was because there could be no future between them anyway. He'd watched her in that café and knew she needed her freedom. He'd never allow someone so beautiful to wither as a prisoner here and that was what would happen. He planned to be the last King of Silvabon and it was a path he had to take alone.

But tonight? As she'd said. He was merely a man. And he couldn't resist her a second longer.

Elsie couldn't believe she was in a vast room so ornate it ought to be monstrous. Yet it wasn't. It was rich and lush and, despite the size, incredibly intimate. That Felipe was so accustomed to such a literally gilded life? He had no idea how uncommon this decadent atmosphere was. But she forgot about the intricately carved wooden crests and glittering crystal chandeliers that made the gold glow because he cupped her face and kissed her—lips, cheekbones, jaw. He leisurely trailed along the base of her neck, gifting her a collar of kisses, licking the pulse of pleasure, exposing her vulnerability and responsiveness to his touch. Delight swirled, building a stronger need. She wanted more. She sank her full weight against him and let him into her mouth, her body…licking him back. She ached for him to take it all. He dropped a hand to stroke her backside and rocked her closer still against him. The rhythm maddened her, pushed her closer to an edge that she couldn't quite grasp. Now she would feel him, have him. Now she would escape this terrible tension. Because it would flow, then ebb, right? Unleashed, it would be explored and then expunged. It had to be, because she was wound so tight she wanted to scream. And he knew. He held her, strong and sure and hard, against his arousal. Her feet parted a little and she pressed again, seeking another rush of pleasure. That pressing need for release bore down on her. Sudden and urgent.

'Elsie.' He felt it. Of course he felt it. 'You want me? Don't be silent.'

He slid his hand to that aching part at the apex of her thighs. It didn't matter that she still wore her dress and panties—that his fingers were blocked by two layers of fabric. But his touch was scorching.

She was so hot, so desperate she was almost in tears. 'Please.'

'Elsie.' His low voice was strained but forceful. 'Take pleasure from me, Elsie.'

She shouldn't have needed his command—his permission—but she did. She'd never let anyone this close. Never *allowed* herself to be this vulnerable, this exposed. She'd never had someone hold her and kiss her and touch her until she lost her mind. She bit her lip, hard.

'I've got you,' he promised.

She let go—a keening high-pitched cry of release as he held her tighter still and slid another luscious drag of his tongue inside her lips. She fell. But he had her. His grip on her tight and sure as she shuddered and bucked against the hot cage of his body. Bolts of pleasure fired through in an orgasm so quick and hard but that left her impossibly hungrier still. And when she opened her eyes and saw his? She felt both a qualm and a resurgence of excitement. He looked as wild as she felt—as tortured by this heat and need. But they were here, now, and he would hold nothing back. That he felt this hunger? That, beneath his perfect royal facade, the man who was dutiful and good was greedy too? That made her breathless and giddy.

He kissed her again and she instantly yielded. She would let him do anything in that moment and he knew it. His sudden smile said it all. He stepped back and she realised he'd unzipped her dress while kissing her senseless. She grabbed the front of the frock before it slithered to the ground. Where a second ago she'd wanted to be naked, now she verged on embarrassment. She'd never been naked in front of *anyone*. But as he lowered his gaze the hunger in his face burnished her returning confidence.

'Drop the dress, Elsie.'

His order fired her blood. 'Pardon?'

'My dauntless rebel.' His smile broadened. 'Drop the damn dress.'

'I'm not going to obey your every command,' she said, resisting the urge to do exactly that. Knowing that his instructions were intended only to please her.

'Oh, but I think you are.' He tugged the front of her dress playfully. 'Just as I'm going to obey yours.'

'Really?' A fierce longing trammelled through her and she couldn't resist testing him. 'Take off your clothes.'

His gaze shot back to hers. 'All of them?'

'Yes.' She swallowed as he stepped back.

She watched, transfixed, as he stripped. A resurgence of arousal struck—she was so close, just from watching him obey her…and the revelation of his beauty? A dangerous smile played around his lips as he unfastened his shirt, then his trousers. He arched his brows as he removed each item—displaying such wicked charm as he laughed in the face of her fierce blushing silence.

He didn't laugh enough—she liked the sound. She wanted to hear it more. But now she drank in the show until he stood before her—naked, strong, proud, fearless. Hers. Everything she *ever* could have wanted. A lithe, strong body—muscular and gleaming and utterly perfect.

'Elsie?' There was a thread of laughter in the steel. 'I think it's your turn.'

She dropped her dress. She was shaking, now clad in nothing but a tiny pair of navy silk knickers and her breasts full and tight and aching for his touch. He flinched and locked his muscles—maximising their already thrilling definition.

She couldn't actually stand any more. He caught her as she trembled.

'Time for bed, sweetheart.' A warning. An order. A release. He stared into her eyes as he lifted her into the centre of his massive bed. His mouth lifted in another lazy smile. 'Time for me.'

Her panties were already damp from the orgasm

he'd wrought from her so easily earlier but with just his words, his expression, her body grew slick and ripe, ready for the possession of his. But it wasn't enough for him, she realised, because he set about kissing every inch of her. He wanted more.

'The scent of you drives me crazy.' Feral hunger sounded in his husky tone. 'I want to taste you too.'

Like an animal. He peeled her panties off and gently stroked her, exposing her to his touch, his tongue, his whole hot, wicked mouth. Gasping, she reached out, caressing the parts of him she could. But he moved down the bed—down her—and licked and nuzzled every centimetre.

'I want to hear you again.' His rhythm was unrelenting, his words driving her wild. 'I want to hear you lose it, Elsie.'

Overwhelmed by the onslaught, she spread her legs wider and arched, exposed in an ultimate invitation. And he ate all she offered. His hands gripped, holding her still as she writhed uncontrollably. Panting and moaning and utterly out of control, she didn't care that she was begging as she came hard for him.

'Now we're here, we have all the time in the world,' he growled.

'We really don't.' Exhausted yet elated, sated yet somehow still starving for more. 'Don't make me wait any longer.'

There was an emptiness inside her. A literal emptiness that she needed him to fill. She wanted him in her arms.

His expression both softened and flickered with satisfaction and amusement. He stroked her hair back from her flushed face. 'I couldn't take my eyes off you that day at the café,' he admitted with a laugh. 'I wanted you here, behind the palace walls.'

He reached in his drawer and pulled out protection.

'You destroyed me before you even spoke,' she mumbled as she watched him prepare himself to take her. 'Before you made me mad. Before you made me laugh. I wanted you and I knew I wasn't going to have you.'

'You can have me now, sweetheart.' He parted her legs so he could push between them. 'And I can have you.'

The hunger in his voice and his gaze made her shiver, made her excitement tighten again. 'Yes. Please.'

The wanton luxuriousness in this most secret of hours made her fearless and bold.

Braced above her, he grazed his knuckles down her body and tested the cleft between her legs once more. 'You're so hot for me,' he groaned.

'Yes.'

He dropped his hips and she felt the first intimate press of him. She was unaccustomed to the weight of any man, let alone a man as tall and muscular as he, but she loved the sense of security—of being pinned in place by him—right at her core. The searing invasion of his rigid body was too slow. She sighed achingly. She wanted him to hold her so close that she couldn't escape. So tight that no one could take her from him. So completely that no one could send her away. Ever. She cried out because that wish was so close—but ultimately impossible.

'Elsie? You with me?' He paused at this most pivotal of moments, his muscles bunching with tension.

'Yes.' The breathiest of whispers as she blinked through the shock and the intensity of her emotions. 'Take me. *Please*.' A raw cry of need.

With a thrust he fully breached both her physical and emotional barriers. She cried out again at the intense, ferocious reality of his possession. He was *hers*. 'Yes,' she sobbed. 'Yes.'

'Elsie.' He huffed a growl as she arched her hips to let him slide that bit further, easier inside her.

He kissed her and moved slowly, taking such care in his caresses, testing her response to his touch, so attuned he adjusted his timing, the depth and intensity of each thrust to make her savour each moment of this discovery...until he aroused her to the point of madness. And he knew—because it was at that exact moment that he grinned at her.

'This what you wanted?' His playfulness returned.

Her heart sang. She wanted to provoke him. In part to hide the emotional intensity of sharing herself with him. She'd not expected this to mean so much. But it did. And she wanted it to be like that for him too. Instinctively she nipped his lower lip the way he'd nipped hers earlier.

'You want it harder?' His eyes sparkled.

'I want *you* out of control.' She was beyond eager to see that, to feel it, to be the cause.

'Be careful what you wish for, Elsie.' A low growl, a glittering tease.

'What are you going to do?' she challenged. 'Tie me down and touch me till I scream?'

He thrust deep inside her and stilled—his eyes drilled as deep as his body. He let his full weight drop on her so she couldn't move. With heart-shuddering ease he clamped his hands around both her wrists and lifted them above her head. There he pinioned them together in the one hand and held them firmly to the mattress. Now she really could barely move.

'I can feel you getting hotter,' he growled. 'And tighter…' He half choked. 'Shouldn't be possible but…*oh*.' He groaned as Elsie quivered with another of those pre-orgasmic clenches she couldn't control.

The slip in his facade when she did that? She realised it was the key to *his* loss of control. She rocked her hips—the slight amount she could—and squeezed on him again.

'Elsie.' A warning this time.

One she was utterly thrilled to ignore. Because while he had her wrists pinned, making her his very willing prisoner, she now lifted her legs and locked them around his hips. And she wasn't letting him go either. He swore with such barely contained savagery, it heated her more. She rocked, using muscles she'd not worked much before, driving him until he took over completely. Lost to the rhythm and the most basic of urges, they pounded together. Her gaze was locked on his, watching the gorgeous agony as he fought to delay the delicious inevitable drowning of reason. Sensation pummelled her as he rolled his hips, pushing harder and deeper and rubbing her right where she needed. As she screamed he released her wrists and hauled her closer. His body shook as his orgasm surged and electrified her own. Hands released, she clutched him so hard she'd leave scratches on his back. But his breath was in her ears. His words. Her name. Over and over.

CHAPTER ELEVEN

Saturday, 02.27 a.m.

ELSIE KEPT HER eyes tightly closed. She didn't want
this to end. She didn't want him to lift off her. Her
breathlessness wasn't from this weight but the mind-
blowing intensity of what she'd just experienced.
But she shivered and he immediately moved and
reached to pull a covering over them. Only he suddenly stopped.

'Elsie?' A soft query.

She *really* didn't want to open her eyes.

'Elsie.' He sounded uncharacteristically uncer-
tain. 'You bled.'

She'd read that not every woman did the first time
they had sex. She'd hoped that would be her, but it
seemed luck wasn't on her side this second. 'Please
let's not make a big deal of it,' she whispered.

'So…' He drew an audible breath. 'Was that…?'
A sigh this time—one that merged with a muttered
imprecation. 'Elsie, was that your first time?'

She was mortified. This was a conversation she'd
hoped to avoid. She'd hoped he wouldn't have noticed. 'Please don't make it matter more than it does.'

*Please don't be angry with me. Please don't
ruin what has been so perfect.*

'Look at me.' He put a hand on her shoulder, a firm one.

She opened her eyes and saw the burdens he carried—wariness and concern—back in his gaze.

'How much does it matter?' he asked, clearly confused. And determined to understand. 'How much does it matter to *you*?'

Her heart thudded. 'What matters,' she replied softly, 'is that you just gave me the most amazing experience of my life.' She wasn't afraid for him to know that truth. 'And I'll treasure it always.'

'I could have—'

She covered his mouth with her hand and shook her head. 'It was perfect. I didn't want you to stop. Please don't be mad.'

He blinked and pulled her hand away, keeping a tight hold of it in his. 'I'm not mad. I'm just…' He drew in a jagged breath. 'I'm sorry you didn't trust me enough to tell me.'

'I trusted you not to hurt me. To take care with me. And I was right. But personal things…'

'You think what just happened wasn't personal?' he countered. 'Why did you give me this? Why for only a few hours, when I can offer you so little in return?'

'Other people do.'

'Other people haven't saved themselves—' He frowned as if she were a puzzle. 'No boyfriend ever, Elsie?'

His surprise made her smile. 'Did you think I'd been having flings all over the continent?'

'Other people do,' he echoed.

'Yeah, well…' She shrugged.

He gazed at her for another long moment. 'Don't you think you're worth an actual relationship?' He tightened his hold as she tried to tug her hand free of his. 'You don't have them, do you? Even friendships. You move places so frequently I don't think it's possible. You won't put down roots. You won't fight to stay in one place. Why?' He gazed right into her eyes. 'You can tell me anything…you know that, right?'

She knew he meant it. But she shook her head. 'I told you, I trust you with my body, Felipe. But my secrets? My thoughts? What's precious to me in here?' She pressed her hand to her heart. 'I don't trust anyone with any of that.'

'Who broke your trust, Elsie?'

She smiled sadly. 'I'd have to trust you to tell you.'

'I won't tell anyone. I won't see you again past sunrise. What's the risk in telling me?'

'What's the reason to?'

He shifted and leaned back against the headboard. 'Because carrying a heavy burden is hard. It's lonely sometimes.'

The throb in his voice she recognised; they were two lonely, isolated people.

'Maybe sharing it might lighten it,' he muttered. 'Even for a little while.'

Her heart ached. 'As if you ever do that?'

A glimmer of an acknowledgement as he smiled. 'Then let's trade.'

She turned to him. 'You're going to trust me with one of your secrets?'

'You know I trust you.' He wrapped his arms around her and drew her back to rest against his chest.

'Even though you didn't read that security check on me?' she asked, stupidly saddened by that realisation. 'Grab your phone. Do it now. You hardly need detective skills—it's all there in a simple search. Type in my name and it pops up like it happened yesterday. It's never going to go away.'

'I'm not going to do that. I'd rather you told me,' he said huskily. 'Start small. Tell me one little thing.'

She laughed. 'You're never going to stop at wanting just one.'

He brushed his hand through her hair. 'One thing and I'll give you a kiss.'

She leaned into the touch. 'Are you *seducing* me into giving up my secrets?'

'Absolutely.' He kissed the base of her neck.

She pulled back and shot him a look. 'One secret. One orgasm.'

'There's my Elsie, raising the bar. Not afraid to challenge me.' A serious glint entered his eye.

'So why didn't you do that the morning you lost your job?'

Elsie stiffened but Felipe tightened his grip on her ever so slightly and pressed.

'Why didn't you march back to the palace and demand to see me? I know you liked it here. I know you were genuinely fond of Amalia. Why didn't you come and tell me and my interfering security team where to go?'

'Because of *you*.' All that low-burning shame bubbled up. 'I had to leave because of you.'

'Because I—'

'Belonged to someone else.' That possessive fire in her belly had raged so intensely it had been scary.

It was so unlike her. She *wasn't* possessive and she certainly had no right to be possessive of him. Yet there it was. An emotion so strong that she couldn't ignore it—not then, not now. But she'd given him so much already tonight, and he had treated it—her—with infinite care. Which suddenly made it too easy to confess everything.

'If I'd stayed, I would've behaved badly and I wouldn't have cared,' she admitted rawly. Her desire for him made her want to do something wrong and she never wanted to become that person. 'I would have *cheated*. I would have hurt someone else. I *never* wanted to be that person. I always promised I'd never be like—' She broke off and breathed out. 'But the temptation of you?'

He'd made her want to be everything she'd fought

hard not to be. Meeting him had unleashed the part within her that didn't give a damn—that was selfish and hungry and uncaring of anything other than getting what she wanted. Like her father and her brother. People who took what they wanted without any scruples.

'So you left without saying goodbye, without fighting. Because you would've become my lover even though you thought I was engaged to someone else?' His chest rose and fell rapidly.

She closed her eyes, mortified. It was a truth she'd not admitted even to herself until now. 'I didn't even know if you wanted—'

'You know I did.' A husky breath. 'I wanted you desperately but I couldn't, and not because of that damned betrothal. But because of the risk to you. I come with a whole country. Paparazzi and a life so public you can never reclaim your privacy. My mother. Amalia's mother. It was terrible for them both. I don't want that for anyone and certainly not you.' He sighed. 'But this now? You deserve so much more than a few hours…'

'I don't. I really don't.'

'Why do you say that? What happened that was so awful?' He watched her for a moment before asking carefully. 'Can you tell me what's on the video?'

She looked at the suppressed concern in his eyes and realised she had to put him at ease. 'It's not… it's not any kind of sex tape and I wasn't physically hurt or anything… It was a personal moment but not *that* kind of personal.'

He released a long, careful breath.

'I played the mandolin for my mother,' she said simply.

His gaze narrowed but he didn't realise what she'd told him. What it meant. She smiled at him. 'I learned the violin for years, but I found the mandolin in her wardrobe one day when I was clearing it out. It belonged to her great-grandmother.'

'It's old, then.'

She nodded. 'I don't know how she put up with me picking out tunes by ear painfully slowly when I first started. I guess it was a distraction.'

'Because she was sick.'

'Cancer, yes. It took a long time.'

'That must have been hard.'

She hadn't spoken of this in so long. But Felipe was quiet and never going to tell. He trusted her, which allowed her to trust him. 'I looked after her. I was happy to. I dropped out of the course I was studying, lost touch with most of my friends. But I did my creative projects at home while caring for her. I loved music, art, baking…silly stuff.'

'Not silly.'

She smiled at him gratefully. 'It's something we shared.'

'Where was your father? Your brother?' He frowned. 'Were they—?'

'My brother, Caleb, was at university. He's older

by a couple of years. My father worked. He struggled. Was absent.' She frowned. 'Actually he wasn't great. He cheated on Mum. He promised me it was a one-off thing. That he'd been stressed. I'd thought it was just…he was lonely and it was hard with Mum having been sick for so long. But it wasn't one lapse. There were times earlier I'd just been too young and naive to be aware of them. My mother protected me from all that. I'd thought that everything was fine. But he was a cheat in every way possible.'

Felipe was still.

'Mum's illness worsened. There was this new medication she could have but it was expensive. My brother set up a crowdfunding page, you know? I made some things even to sell to raise the money. And we got some in. Quite a bit. But one day right near the end…' She closed her eyes. 'I'd written a song for Mum. It was just for her. From me to her. She was so frail and I didn't know…'

He stiffened. 'Elsie?'

'I didn't know Caleb secretly recorded me the first time I played it for her,' she whispered. The only time. 'He uploaded it to the site—to solicit more donations. It got attention. It got a lot of money. Really quickly. Far more than we needed because by then…' It had come too late for her mother. Elsie still felt so cold, so hurt to think of it. 'Dad and Caleb said they were setting up a foundation to raise more money for other sufferers. I believed them— Caleb was studying accounting, you know? But next thing Caleb arrives in an expensive new car. My dad has a new watch…and Mum had died.'

'Oh, Elsie.' His arms tightened about her.

'I finally figured it out. I went to the police. Testified against them. They faced fraud charges and were sentenced to prison. Caleb's out now. Turned out Dad had been embezzling from his business as well so he's still in there.'

'And you'd lost not only your mother.' He gazed into her eyes. 'But your music.'

'I couldn't play at all for a long time. It was only…'

'Here.'

Yes, on Silvabon. In the sunshine, sitting at the back of the café on a break, looking at the sapphire-blue water. She'd finally begun to defrost and to hear fragments of melody in her mind. Her music had returned. Some of it, at least. And then Amalia had appeared and she'd needed it too.

'I can't play that song at all any more,' Elsie whispered.

It had been taken from her. The precious moment between her and her mother hadn't just been commoditised, it had been used to *con* people out of their money. And as a result, *she'd* been abused in more than one way. Something that had been secret and special had been exposed for public scrutiny and, ultimately, mockery. The glowing compliments had turned as the truth of the money funnelling had emerged. Critics of her composition had shredded her. But it hadn't been intended for anyone else. She wasn't a performer like that. Maybe it had been a little sweet, but not 'falsely saccharine'—like the scathing assessments.

Calculated to pluck your heart strings and open your purse.

'I didn't know he'd recorded it.' She blinked fiercely. 'I didn't know he was going to use it like that.'

'That was the violation of your trust, Elsie,' Felipe said roughly. 'That was the betrayal right there.'

Shame filled her when she thought of it. Shame and such devastation.

'They stole that moment from you,' he muttered. 'I'm so sorry.'

She swiped away the tear. 'Please don't watch it.'

'I won't.'

'Promise?'

'Yes.'

The online pile-on had been horrific and the face-to-face vitriol? Even from people she'd thought were friends. People she'd thought would have her back and believe her. It had made her so wary of other people now. Because it was still there—online, as fresh as the day it had been posted. It would be there for ever.

'I turned my own father and my own brother in, but other people didn't believe that I didn't know. They all doubted me. And my father was so angry when he'd found out I'd gone to the police. He tried to smash my mandolin. That's why the case is broken. He didn't know I'd taken the instrument out and that was only by chance. That's the only reason it survived.'

He'd tried to destroy the last thing she had of her mother's. The thing most precious to her. All in a vitriolic rage.

'We'd never had much money and suddenly people were giving buckets of it. Dad was so greedy. He thought it was a way of getting more without having to work for it. By lying to people.'

'He lied to you too.'

Yeah. He'd monetised what should have been a bittersweet, heart-rending but precious memory. Put it out there for people to judge and mock.

'It didn't matter that I'd been honest. Everyone had judged me anyway. Sometimes I think it would have been easier to say nothing.'

'Doing the right thing takes courage.'

'Was it the right thing though? Was it worth all that upheaval? It didn't make anything better. It didn't mean those people were *repaid*.' She was mortified that they'd lost money.

'But they saw that justice was done. That matters. We need to see that. We need to know there are good people in the world.' Felipe regarded her solemnly. 'But you always worry how they'll react if, when, they find out?'

'No one likes a nark, right?' She glanced at him. 'No one believes that I couldn't have known sooner.

How could I not have known? I even made things to auction for the fundraiser. I was so *stupid*.'

'Not stupid. Sweet and sincere. And you are not responsible for the choices your father and brother made.'

'Family sticks together. Family doesn't rat each other out. They disowned me completely,' she said. 'My father's family won't forgive me.'

'There's nothing to forgive, Elsie. You did the right thing. You shouldn't be paying for their mistakes.'

But she was. 'My mother was an only child so there's no one there. And all my old friends didn't just doubt me, they didn't believe me. I don't belong to anyone or to any place. Not any more.'

'So now you're alone and now you don't trust anyone.' He swept his hand through her hair. 'I won't let you down.'

'There's no time for that to happen.' She tried to smile but found she couldn't.

His arm around her waist tightened. 'There's nothing wrong with wanting touch and connection. You shouldn't ever feel as if you shouldn't have that.' He sighed. 'And you should have so much more than this.'

'I'm scared I'd want *too* much,' she whispered harshly. 'If I let it go, let it consume me? I could be the most jealous witch.' She already was. 'That's what scares me—being as selfish and as greedy as them.'

'You wouldn't. That fear is from the threat of losing it, right? That it was going to be taken away from you. Another time, another place, another...' He whistled in a raspy breath. 'You'll find the security that you deserve. You're nothing like your father Elsie. You're not dishonest. You're not a cheat. You didn't. And you wouldn't ever. You need to forgive yourself. You did nothing wrong. They let you down and they shouldn't have. But you shouldn't suffer any punishment. You should have a home and a job and a family—whatever you want, with someone you want. You should have it all.'

But not with him. With some other guy some other time. And that thought? *No.*

She was exposed and she needed—*escape*. She appreciated Felipe's sentiment. She didn't even regret telling him about her family, but she slid from the bed, taking the top sheet with her. Because she couldn't stay in his arms telling him all her secrets. Soon she'd be begging him never to let her go. This wasn't that and never would be.

'Where are you going?' he asked.

'I'm annoyed with you.'

He sat up, startled. 'Why?'

'You should have it all too.' She shot him a look. 'You think that's possible for me, but not for yourself.'

His jaw compressed. 'I'm not in the same position as most people, Elsie. Not even most other royals. There's *only* me.'

'Is that what your grandfather said?' Honestly, she didn't much like the sound of the old man.

'I'm the last one.'

She snorted. 'That's impossible. The King is dead, long live the King, right?'

He drew a breath. 'Not yet. There's no clear successor. It's on me to declare one.'

'Or have an heir of your own—your own children.'

'Not happening.'

She looked back at him, realising he was utterly serious. 'So when you die…'

'The monarchy will become extinct. Our elected representatives will have full power. We'll become a democratic republic.'

She gaped. 'But Silvabon loves its monarchy.' They loved *him*. 'They won't let it happen. Won't let some distant cousin crawl out of the woodwork, claim the crown and cause all sorts of chaos.'

'Not if I say there's no crown anymore. Not if I've relinquished the excessive power the Crown currently has.'

That was what he planned to do? Elsie was shocked. 'But you could choose to appoint someone—'

'No.' He flashed a tight smile. 'I'm not declaring a successor.'

No children? No successor? 'Because you think it's a poisoned chalice?' She frowned, not understanding him at all. 'But you're so popular. Everyone loves you and you do *all* those things.' She'd seen it in all the coverage—the effort he went to for his country, promoting his people, the causes. 'You *love* it here.'

'I do,' he said simply. 'I want nothing but the best for Silvabon. And I will do nothing but my best *for* it.'

'Then to leave the country without a monarch when it's such a part of…?' She slowly shook her head. 'Can nobody better *you*, Felipe?'

A husky, bitter laugh. 'You don't agree with my plan?'

'No. I don't.' She slowly climbed the curling wooden staircase. 'You're so arrogant, Felipe. Can no one else help you? No one keep you company to help shoulder the burden and keep you warm?'

'I have too much power.' His gaze narrowed. 'You don't understand what—'

'Oh, I understand. The great King Felipe. Determined to be an isolated martyr to the end…'

His jaw dropped and she laughed at the expression in his eyes.

'Lie there and listen to the truth, Felipe. If you're so trapped, I guess you're stuck there?'

She was suddenly angry with *both* of their circumstances and she didn't want to waste any more of their precious minutes dwelling on things that couldn't—or wouldn't—be changed. She could have it *all* tonight but *only* tonight. And it seemed it was the same for him.

Felipe stared in shock as this *nymph* ascended the curling wooden staircase with a dramatic flair he should've anticipated sooner. His body was hard and his heart? Racing.

'King Felipe,' she said softly. 'The man who sacrifices everything for his country.'

'What are you *doing*?' His heart wouldn't stop pounding and her fiery reaction was confusing the hell out of him.

'I've had enough *talking*.'

Oh. But he was hurt for her—for what her family had done. For her losses. But now? Now she'd flipped on him and she was full of fury and strength and he wanted her. 'Then come back down here.'

He'd been the one to scoff at virgin princess brides, yet she'd been innocent and her naive assumption revealed she was a believer in fairy tales. This wasn't going to be one. But he also knew she understood that. Hence, *this*.

Now she'd hit the balcony and she peeked over the railing. Her skin flushed. 'Oh. Okay.'

'What?'

'It's a really great view.'

'Is it?' He couldn't resist stretching out on the bed for her.

'Are you putting on a show for me?'

Amusement lit him up all over. 'Would you like me to?'

She glanced down his body. 'I think that could be pretty good.'

'Then absolutely, I will give you a show.' He

stretched wide then ran his hands across his chest before sliding them south, massaging his thighs, then…

'Maybe you should stop…' Her voice wobbled.

'Not sure I can.' He could see she was excited. Hell, *he* was excited. To teach her more. To make it better. In this one way, this one night maybe he could…but how could it get better than what they'd shared just before?

'You'd better,' she called down to him.

'Or what?'

'Or…' She bit her lip, a gesture not of wariness but of sensuality. 'I'll have to make you pay.'

He was absolute toast. She was going to toy with him and he was going to let her. She watched, fascinated, as he slowly stretched his hand back onto the mattress.

'Good.' She stood at the top of the staircase and slowly let the sheet fall from her body until she was as naked as he.

She was watching him with a fixated, glazed look and he knew she was dreaming of what she was about to do to him.

'I think you'd better get ready for me,' she said.

Felipe could hardly don protection, his fingers were trembling so much.

She sashayed down the stairs, back to him. She didn't ask with words, but discovered with her hands his most sensitive places. He liked it when she made the decisions, had liked it when she'd lain back and let him decide everything too. He was used to people paying attention to him—waiting for his command, seeking his advice, doing his bidding. But this was different. This was Elsie taking time to know him. Taking what she wanted. Their push and pull, give and take were intoxicating. He could boss her in a way he'd not dared with another only because she liked to flip and push it back on him. So he let it happen now—let her tease him. Her concentration was the sexiest thing he'd ever seen. There was an almost gauche generosity to her actions. But she was doing this not only to please him but to sate her own curiosity as well. Not because she thought she had to pleasure him, but because she truly wanted to. He felt utterly honoured and it was a gift he didn't take for granted. He wanted to gift her more in return and he couldn't hold back any more. He reached for her.

'For once in your life, let someone else take charge,' she hissed at him. 'Hold onto the headboard.'

He stared at her. 'Is that an order?'

'Absolutely.'

His muscles sharpened. 'You know I'll get you back for this.'

'I'm aware. And I'll accept that as my due reward.' A sweet, sweet whisper.

He could hardly breathe, and he couldn't release the board above his head now. If he did, he'd clutch her so hard he'd bruise her. His need for her was white-hot and blinding. His arms burned.

His whole body was tense—as if he were on the damned rack and being stretched—just waiting for her to claim him.

Elsie stared down at him. Felipe was a beautiful, beautiful man and tonight he was hers. She released everything—the kind of hunger she'd never allowed to flow. That truly she'd never felt before. All-consuming, yet so playful.

'Hold on,' she muttered, while holding *him* her prisoner by straddling his powerful thighs. But she didn't take him yet. She teased and took him in her hands.

'I am,' he gritted. 'I will.'

She felt liberated and free and giddy with desire.

'Elsie,' he groaned. 'What are you doing?'

'I'm playing you. Do you like it?'

'Your fingers are magical.'

She giggled breathlessly. 'Hardly.'

'Trust me, they're amazing.'

'You want me to play you some more?'

'Mmm-hmm.' He strained into her hand.

'Oh.' Pleased, she shimmied closer. 'What other pretty sounds can we extract from you?'

'Pretty sounds?' he gasped with mock outrage. A groan swiftly followed.

She laughed. The power of this, the play, was everything. The smile he sent her, the growls of delight, another groan of exquisite agony. She loved it all.

'Elsie.'

That was what she liked best. His desperate, help-less muttering of her name. She blew on his hot skin, gently exploring him. He was her perfect instrument, big and strong, and he bent to her touch and arched into her hands, making her feel all-powerful. She liked it so much she hummed her own pleasure in seeking out his.

'You're killing me.'

'I think you're very much alive, Felipe.'

'Ride me.' He swore again and thrust his hips upwards. 'Ride me.'

An order, but she chose to take it as a plea. Slowly she sank onto him—adoring the glazed look in his eyes as he stared from her flushed face, down her body.

'Not sore?' He gasped desperately.

'I'm fine,' she assured him. 'More than fine.'

His obvious relief made her bolder and sink deeper, even more pleasurably. That was when he struck. He released the headboard and sat up swiftly. Clasping her to his chest, he kissed her and kissed her and he didn't let her go. Not until she'd come again. And again. Not even when she finally collapsed and succumbed to sleep.

CHAPTER TWELVE

Saturday, 04.37 a.m.

FELIPE WOKE, TENSION rippling through his body as he realised how many hours they'd lost. He needed time to stop. He didn't want his valet arriving in an hour. He didn't want to send her away. He wasn't ready.

'I fell asleep,' he muttered. 'Damn.'

She lifted her head from where it was nestled in the side of his neck and drowsily smiled. 'You needed it. You have a big day ahead. You don't want to be so tired you're slurring your words in front of the world.'

He didn't want to think about the world right now. But there was no stopping the reality speeding towards them.

'Your fellow plane passengers are going on a tour at nine,' he said, trying to lighten his own mood. 'So I'm not totally wasting their precious time with my unreasonable detainment of them.'

Her ice-blue eyes softened. 'A tour?'

'I'll have you know we got a one hundred per cent strike rate on the offer.'

'I bet you did. I would've said yes to a tour like that.'

'I'll give you a private tour right now if you like,' he said huskily. 'The best Silvabon has to offer.'

Her eyebrows arched. 'The best?'

'The *very* best.' He threw back the sheet and forced himself out of bed. 'And just so you know, I'm *never* redecorating this room.' He lifted his finger. 'That viewing balcony stays. In fact, I can think of some enhancements.'

'Enhancements?' She laughed. 'And are you going to impregnate your wife in front of an audience like the good old days?'

He shot her a look. 'You know I'm not going to have a wife to impregnate.'

She shook her head disbelievingly.

'Stop trying to marry me off,' he said. 'I'll release most of the power the Crown currently has over the next few years. Then I'll grow old and slowly become nothing more than a figurehead. After I'm gone this place will become a museum.'

'It should never be a museum. It should be filled with life and footsteps and laughter.' She slapped down the plans he'd taken so long to prepare. 'Why not become a figurehead *family*, doing positive things for the country?'

Oh, she did still believe in fairy tales. 'The personal cost is too great,' he said honestly.

'And your decision to remain alone isn't a personal cost?'

'It's not for *me*.' He smiled now. 'I've known no different.'

She stared into his eyes. 'Your children would

know no different from the royal life you create for them.'

'I'm *never* having…' He stiffened. 'I'm not doing that to them—being born into such a burden? That's not fair.'

'Yet that's what happened to you and you're still here and you even told me you love it. So why wouldn't they?'

Because no one else *had* stayed. Because he couldn't take the risk of their unhappiness.

'Maybe if there was a solid support structure?' Elsie offered tentatively. 'Maybe, yeah, release some power so they were more free to do the work they're passionate about? Maybe then it could be okay?'

'It's not that easy.'

'Nothing great ever is. But wouldn't it be worth trying? To have a family flourish in this crazy huge palace? How wonderful would that be…? Surely you could insist on more balance? Royals in other places seem to.'

Seem to was the thing, but protocol was ingrained and *people* were too complicated and couldn't be stretched too far. *He* couldn't do balanced—it wasn't in his genes. They were all or nothing and he couldn't put anyone else through it or ask them to make such sacrifice.

'Real life isn't that simple.' He drew breath, desperate to end the fantasy she was tempting him with. 'Come on, hurry up.'

They were losing too much time.

'I'm not sure if this has registered with you, but I'm naked right now.'

'It has registered, actually.' He grinned. 'I like it.'

'Yeah, well, if you want us to sneak around the palace like rebellious teenagers, then you might want to find us something to wear. I'll probably get caught on the security cameras and I don't need any more unflattering footage up on the Internet.'

With an exasperated growl he went into his dressing room and returned wearing black shorts and holding a white tee shirt. He ripped the tag off it and handed it to her.

'You have a wardrobe full of new clothes?'

'You already know I'm spoilt. No need to judge harder.'

'I'm not. I'm delighted. It's very handy this second.' She slid the tee on; it hung on her like a dress.

He stared at her. 'You can make literally anything look good.'

She flushed. 'Stop charming me.'

The only thing he wanted to stop right now was time and that was impossible even for him. 'Let's go.'

'Where?'

'There are over a thousand rooms in this castle, did you know that?' He winked at her. 'That's not counting the secret ones.'

'A *thousand* rooms and you choose that theatre to sleep in?' She laughed as she followed him down the corridor. 'Honestly, Felipe.'

'You have to admit it has its benefits…'

'Your *enhancements* should include silk ropes. You could hang them from the balcony railing,' she provoked him slyly. 'Work on a naked aerial circus act…'

Silk ropes? He turned back and saw the playful gleam in her eyes. 'That's a stunning idea.'

'Thank you.' Elsie almost had to run to keep up with him. The corridor was narrow and barely lit and had lost all the luxury palace feel. This part was pure hand-hewn stone. He paused by an oak door.

'What's this?' she asked, aware of the vitality and anticipation in his gorgeous eyes.

'My secret. It was a trade, right? I'm looking forward to my reward orgasm already.' He opened the door.

'Your—' She broke off and stared at the view he'd just exposed. The door led to a ledge on the edge of a cliff. The sapphire sea gleamed metres below. 'Don't tell me you—'

'Cliff-jump? Absolutely.'

Her heart raced. 'I thought you weren't a risk taker. You're jumping into the open sea and have to avoid those rocks.' She glanced down at the water and then back at him worriedly. 'They're big rocks, Felipe.'

'And I've managed to avoid them every day for the last decade. Trust me. It looks harder and scarier than it is. It's actually easy. You game?'

She really wasn't. But she wasn't going to say no. This was their one night—and it was barely light. She could have a few more moments. 'Are there sharks?'

He chuckled. 'Hold my hand, I'll get us into the right spot.'

She held his hand. Hard. The water was a shock and she let go of him, gasping as she surfaced.

'I didn't think it would be this *cold*!' She glared at him indignantly when he laughed. 'I thought it would be like a bath. The beach is so much warmer than this.'

'Because the water here is deeper.' He swam towards her with energy and a huge smile. 'And it's very early. And you were hot from being in bed.'

'I'm not hot now.'

'Sure you are. That shirt has gone devastatingly transparent.' He stretched out his arm and tugged her nearer. 'This way.'

They swam a short distance past the rock and she realised there was a cave entrance tucked below where they'd jumped.

Felipe put both palms on the rock and vaulted from the water, turning to extend a hand to help her out. 'Come on, Elsie, welcome to my dungeon.'

'Oh. *Wow*.'

There were worn stone stairs and as she climbed them the hidden cave's interior fully came into view. And when he flicked a switch?

'Wow!'

How was there electricity down here? She wriggled her toes. How were there large smooth marble tiles beneath her feet that were warm? And was that round pool built into the back of the small cave *steaming*?

'The thermal water is piped to give the cave some heat.'

She knew there were hot springs on other parts of the island and a public facility in the centre of the city, but to have his private pool?

'From here the palace has private access to the open sea—as long as you know how to get past those big rocks,' he explained. 'Originally it was rumoured the King's treats were smuggled in under cover of darkness—straight from the sea.'

'Treats? You mean like cigars and brandy? *Women?*'

'It's never been verified.' He smiled. 'Then they started the story that the dungeons were down here. That there are torture chambers and that people disappeared from here. It was a plan to keep people afraid and away. But, in fact, only the King's most trusted warriors were permitted in. This was their place to heal battle wounds—to rest and recuperate in privacy and hewn comfort.'

She touched the stone. 'So it's really old.'

'The worn mosaics didn't give it away?' He laughed. 'It was abandoned for a long time. I came here as a kid. Then after my father left, I got it cleaned up. Put in some lighting.'

'Because you have a spare chandelier or two lying round,' she teased lightly. 'Not to mention a few nice rugs and fancy cushions.'

'We added in a fridge and a little oven as well.'

'You can use an oven? You amaze me.' She chuckled. But the thought of him restoring this place intrigued her. When there were over a thousand rooms to choose from in that palace, he'd still wanted his own space. 'Your grandfather didn't know you jumped off that cliff, did he?'

'No.'

'Free-diving for pearls, cliff-jumping to access caves. You love the water. Rebel Felipe.'

He shrugged slightly. 'Only my valet and my top security men know. And now you.'

She was incredibly touched about that—too touched. She needed to deflect the emotion that suddenly surged. 'They helped carry the fridge?'

He laughed softly. 'Yeah.'

She studied the bookcase that was tucked beside the cleverly concealed fridge and oven. 'It's literally your man cave.'

But there were no giant screens. Just books and an exercise area on the other side of the pool. This revealed such a secret side to him that she couldn't resist exploring. The books were fiction mostly— crime and fantasy, witches and dragons and great battles. Several looked as if they'd fallen into that great big bath more than once. It seemed he appreciated imagination—and she knew he had a playful one of his own. This place was his private escape.

'You bathe here every morning?'

'Sometimes in the evening as well.'

Alone. Because he was locked in his palace—a young king burdened by responsibility, expectation and isolation. It saddened her. 'You never had wild teen parties down here?'

'No orgies either, before you ask. And I know you were going to ask.'

'Then what's with the massage oil?' She picked up a small bottle and waggled it at him.

'That's from when I had a sore calf from running too much once.' He lifted a shoulder. 'The water has healing properties. The trick is alternating the cold sea with the thermal spring. Which we need to do now because you're shivering.'

Shivering not just from cold, but from deepening heartache. She turned to hide it and climbed the curling stairs into the perfect pool tucked at the back of the cave. The warm water soothed her sensitive skin. She studied the beautiful veined patterns on the ancient marble tiles as the chandelier cast a golden glow in the gloomy space. The bubbling of the endless spring echoed softly against the rocky walls. She knew the islands cradled a wealth of natural resources but this was pure magic.

She glanced over and saw he was watching her with a softly wicked smile.

'Do you like my torture chamber, my darling?' he teased.

Like it? She never wanted to leave it. But she couldn't admit that. 'It's not bad, though I think you've wrecked the vibe with those kettle-bell weights.'

Felipe chuckled and pulled her towards him. 'Down here no one can hear you scream.'

But she couldn't scream because he was kissing her. And when he kissed her, time stopped. She *never* wanted him to stop kissing her.

Somehow they were out of that pool. She lay in a tumble of soft cushions and he massaged her with the oil and she was thankful he'd brought protection in his swim shorts. The scent of cedar and sandalwood and bay filled her—earthy and fresh and heated. Afterwards, warmth from the heated stone rose through the rug where she lay sleepily. But through the rocky fissure masking the cave's entrance she saw the glimpse of sky lighten and the sea begin to sparkle.

Time threatened. 'Thank you for sharing your secret place with me,' she said.

She was beautiful, lying on his rug, gleaming in the golden light. Felipe wanted to demand she stay for ever. His secret treat, hidden down here for always. But that was impossible and he couldn't stop time any more than he could stop that thermal spring or those waves hitting the cliffs.

'You're frowning.' She smoothed his forehead. 'Are you nervous for the coronation?'

He shook his head. 'I'm used to it.'

'But this is really big.'

'Are you trying to *make* me nervous?' He laughed.

But she turned those eyes on him. 'Don't you ever wish you could just get in a boat and head out of here?'

'Disappear in the middle of the night?' He glanced to that gap where he could see the sea. 'No. I would never do that to Silvabon. Not after my father.'

The truth of his abdication was a long-kept secret but now his father and grandfather were gone. There was no need to protect them any more. Felipe was tired of protecting them. 'We woke up one morning and he was missing. That's why my security chief is so paranoid now. He missed my father's escape. Grandfather was apoplectic that he could've left without anyone knowing.'

'You mean he literally ran away? Like, "escaped the dungeon" sort of ran away?'

Felipe nodded. 'He left a two-line apology on a piece of palace paper. He didn't want to be stuck here. Both Grandfather and my mother knew he was restless, it wasn't a complete surprise to them—only that he got out with such secrecy and skill.'

'Was it a surprise to you?'

He stilled. 'I knew they weren't happy. I didn't know about her.'

'Amalia's mother?'

'She was a musician at a club in town. A single woman with a baby. You can imagine how that went down with my grandfather. And the media made it so much worse. They ignored her talent, belittling her as a trampy showgirl. She was vilified. As was my mother—the frigid wife who couldn't satisfy her husband. They're always particularly harsh on women. I don't want that for Amalia. Or anyone.'

'Where's Amalia's father?'

'Long gone. Apparently he didn't want to be a dad and left before she was born.'

'So Amalia understands what it's like to be abandoned too.'

Felipe's heart puckered at the realisation. 'Yeah, I guess she does.'

He had more in common with his stepsister than he'd ever have imagined.

Elsie nodded. 'I didn't know your father just disappeared.'

'My grandfather kept the story quiet while he tried to bully him into coming home.' He sighed. 'But that didn't work. My father had got far enough away to make his escape complete. And when everyone found out? The news cycle fed off it for months—demanding answers that were never given. They still bring it up regularly.'

'And your mother?'

Was destroyed. 'Went to one of the smaller islands.'

'Did you go with her?'

'I was needed here. I was now next in line to the Crown and Grandfather had a lot to teach me. They decided the investiture was the best way to change the narrative from the runaway royal escaping the tyrant King...'

She looked troubled. 'You were separated from both your parents.'

'That's not as miserable as it might sound. They were wrapped up in their own affairs.' He felt bitterness flicker. 'I couldn't console my mother anyway.'

'You shouldn't have had to. She should have been here for you.'

'Grandfather blamed her for not keeping my father happy. She couldn't handle his anger and she's never got over it.' She'd been betrayed so publicly, blamed by his grandfather, rejected. Felipe had hidden his own anxiety, loneliness, heartache from her. 'I was old enough to handle it. Besides, I wasn't the target of his anger. I was his hope for the future.'

'But she's not coming to your coronation today?'

'I told you, she vowed never to set foot in the palace again.'

'Not at all—when you were younger?' Elsie asked. 'Not even now your grandfather is dead?'

'She can't live in the public eye, Elsie,' he said firmly. 'Her nerves can't take it and I don't expect her to. We talk on the phone. I visit her...'

'You do all the work for everyone. All the caretaking. Even for the country itself,' Elsie murmured. 'Did your father ever return?'

'He wasn't allowed. He'd made his choice. It wasn't here.' It wasn't him. 'They went to Canada. The three of them built a new life. A private one.'

'So he didn't come back.' She leaned closer. 'Did you ever visit them?'

He glanced down. 'That would have been a security risk. Plus, Grandfather didn't want my father influencing me away from my duty.'

Her eyes widened. 'You never saw your father again?'

'Not in person. No.' Felipe watched the small patch of sky beyond the rocks brighten with a sinking feeling. 'I think he was happy over there. That's why it's hard for me to have brought Amalia here. I know this isn't what they'd have wanted for her.'

'It sounds like he missed you,' Elsie said. 'He obviously talked to Amalia about you a lot.'

Yeah. He was still getting his head around that. It felt both good and bitter and just…sad.

'That's why I won't give her an honorary title or make her a princess. It's important she knows she can do anything, be anything, go anywhere once she's of age.'

'But you'll still teach her to dive, right?'

Honestly, he was still a little thrown by that request.

'She obviously chose those pearls last night because she'd heard about them—and you—from your dad,' Elsie said. 'You must have missed him too.'

He bent his head. He did not want to think about this, let alone *feel*.

'I know you feel an immense duty to protect her,' Elsie said. 'But she also needs family, Felipe. *Everyone* does.'

'Family isn't always awesome. You know that.'

'But *you're* pretty awesome. And you and Amalia could be a small but strong family, right? Can't families be fixed sometimes?' she said wistfully. 'Can't we rebuild them?'

It was too late. And it was too complicated. Because there were elements in his life that no one else should have to shoulder. He'd seen how much it damaged those who didn't have the desire to handle it.

'I'm sorry, Felipe. They weren't here for you. None of them. Not for *you*.' She sighed, her frown deepening as she tried to understand. 'Your parents' marriage wasn't arranged, was it?'

'No, it was a love match that didn't last. That's why my grandfather was so keen for me to keep the betrothal with Sofia. He thought a political alliance between two professional royals would be better.'

'And you kept it up to keep him happy. Until?' She pressed her lips together.

'Until I realised it wasn't fair on Sofia or anyone else. Not even me.' He was better off on his own.

'Not going to lie, Felipe, the Javier dude doesn't sound like he was all that great.'

Felipe tried to laugh. Tried to explain. 'He wasn't that bad, you know? For a long time he was a good king. And he wanted what was best for everyone. For the country. But then he got older and he was more sick than we realised, I guess. He was losing his grip on his mind so he tightened his grip elsewhere even more. He got really difficult in the final years. Some parts of his mind faded, while he fixated on certain things.' On lineage. On the Crown. On Felipe. 'The courtiers wanted to keep his cognitive decline under wraps for as long as possible because of my age and the risk of political instability. If others thought the King was incapacitated in any way…' It was why he was going to clear the bulk of the King's power and change the constitution. 'I took on most of the public engagements. It's why I'm in that ridiculous bedroom. That historic wing of the palace was the easiest to make most secure. We converted his rooms into a full facility hospital suite and created an enrichment area to try to slow the advancing dementia…'

'You cared for him.'

'Of course. I had to stay here for him. I was the only one left who could. And he was a good man. Things were just different. He'd had a happy marriage. His wife had died young and he wanted stability for the family and he didn't get it. He didn't understand my father. Honestly, I didn't either…'

'How old were you when he got ill?'

'Almost twenty.'

'So soon after your father left? You were so young. And you were trapped here.' She gazed at him. 'Not just by duty and obligation. You were *literally* trapped.'

No, he wasn't. 'I was being *protected*. And then I was protecting him. And my country.'

'Felipe.' She shook her head. 'No. What they did to you?' She drew in a shaky breath. 'When did you last leave—last take a holiday?'

'It's not possible to leave for any length of time. I couldn't let them down. They need me to be here.' Defensiveness rose. He'd never allowed himself to consider leaving for longer.

'Is that what they said?'

His aides, sure. Over and over. 'I was the strong one who had what it took. I was the only one left. Grandfather was counting on me. Not just Grandfather. The whole country.'

'But they left you alone to face everything—including him. Alone, Felipe. They made you become this…'

He stiffened. 'This *what*?'

'Isolated guy. You've had to be so strong. And silent.' She shook her head. 'I don't think anyone should be forced to stay somewhere. Or forced to leave. You should have had *choices*—the freedom to come and go as you wished. To become the person you wanted to be. To have *all* the things. Not just the palace and the power and the people who run at the lift of your little finger. But you should have the family support—the *fun*, companionship, the fulfilment of private and personal dreams...'

He tried to smile at her—to lighten this because it was too intense. Private and personal dreams? 'Don't pity me, Elsie. I already warned you.'

'That you'll use it to ask all the things of me?' She leaned forward. 'Then do it, Felipe. Ask me anything. I would do anything for you. Not because you're the King—because it's *you*.'

He froze, overcome by a desire so strong, so impossible. 'Don't...'

He didn't mean to mutter it. Didn't mean to show how much her words affected him. How much he couldn't handle this. Her sweet generosity? Didn't she know he would take *everything* if he could? Not just sex. She was afraid of being selfish, she had nothing on *his* latent greed.

She read his tension. 'You can tell me *anything* you like. The best. The worst. Just tell me the truth.'

'It wasn't that awful, Elsie.'

'Wasn't it? Are you not *alone*, Felipe?'

He heard the note in her voice. Yeah, she knew how hard that could be—not all the time, but sometimes in those moments when he wasn't quite strong enough... It could be so hard.

'I'm not someone else you have to be strong for and take care of,' she said earnestly. 'Not someone you have to protect.'

'Is that what you think I do?' He tried to pull together some anger. Some humour. Anything to hide from the raw honesty he'd accidentally revealed.

'You did for your grandfather. And your father—you took on his burden, allowing him to escape. And your mother too. Now Amalia. You don't need to be that person for me as well. I mean it. I've been through fire and out the other side. I'm burnished. Tough. I can survive anything. You don't need to protect me. Certainly not here. Definitely not now. So I repeat, you don't need to be strong for me.'

'What should I be, then?'

'You don't have to be *anything* for me. You can just be. You. As you are.'

As you are. He stretched out a hand and ran his finger along the base of her beautiful neck, feeling the delicate notch between her collarbones.

She leaned into his touch, letting him feel her vulnerability and her vitality. 'I mean it.'

'I know you do.' His chest ached. 'Then let's just be.'

No pressure. No expectation. No. It was impossible. And there was no point in talking. It wasn't going to change anything. It was only wasting the precious little time they had left. Only making him feel unsettled.

He kissed her, desperately seeking the mindlessness of physical pleasure. Only it wasn't mindless. There was still thought. Still feeling that went so much deeper than skin on skin. She offered something that couldn't co-exist in his world—a fantasy that could never be real. His country was in his blood. Work was everything and was utterly inextricable from who he was. *What* he was was *who* he was. There was no separating the royal from the man. The duty from the body. But he would never be able to come down here again without thinking of her. Without remembering her silken heat. Without reliving this—the last time they'd made love.

She was shaking but he was too. Both were desperate to go fast, to go slow, to conquer time. They would go back inside the palace. He'd get into his robes and she would leave for good. But right now the emotion in her eyes? He couldn't stand seeing the emotion in her eyes.

'Stop thinking,' he ordered. 'Stop feeling sorry for me.'

Stop feeling anything for me. Suddenly—too late—he realised just what a mistake he'd made.

'How do I do that?' Elsie asked brokenly, torn apart by the sensual, emotional onslaught.

How could she possibly stop thinking? How could she hide her heartbreak knowing, breathing…this was the last time she would hold him? How could she convey everything she was feeling?

It was only so intense because it was the last time, right? She tried to rationalise the ache in her heart. It couldn't happen again.

But it wasn't that. It was more.

Only she couldn't tell him. He'd just told her not to. He wouldn't accept it. And he was far more vulnerable than she ever could've imagined. His father had left him. So had his mother. While his grandfather pressed the weight of a nation's future onto his shoulders—and then became an additional burden on Felipe himself.

He growled, frustration evident in the lines bracketing his mouth, in the tension in his limbs. They kissed with such longing. So close there was no room left any more for thought. Only feeling. Only letting him in—so deeply, intensely, her heart soared. If there was only this, this was complete. She wrapped around him. She never wanted him to let her go. She never wanted to let *him* go.

There was no more talking. Then there was no more time.

Silently he stood and held his hand out to help her up. The robe he fetched was huge on her and clearly his.

He wrapped a towel around his waist and rubbed his forehead. 'Elsie—'

'I need you to get me to my room,' she muttered.

'I'll get you there but you can't leave the palace yet.' He shot her an apologetic look. 'Media crews are already in place. You'll be driven out in the convoy of the other VIPS and dignitaries. Ortiz will get you to the airport safely.'

Her throat was growing tighter and tighter. 'Do I have to scale that cliff?'

'There's a secret passageway from here.'

She silently followed him through a long narrow corridor until he paused at a doorway.

'Go through, yours is the second on the left. I'll stay in here.'

This was it. Would he give her a goodbye kiss as he moved from one stage of his life to the next?

No. He remained standing at a distance, stared at her hard, resolute.

If he asked she would stay. Here. Hidden. His. She would stay in this secret part of the palace. She would do anything for him. Always.

But he didn't ask. And she didn't ask either. Neither said goodbye. She couldn't make a sound. She took the step and heard the door close behind her. And then she realised what she'd done.

She'd left him. Just like everyone else.

CHAPTER THIRTEEN

Saturday, 09.42 a.m.

ELSIE PACED IN her suite. Her heart thudded, trying to escape her ribcage. She had to get out of here but she couldn't. When she'd snuck in early this morning, she'd found her meagre luggage in the corner. Her mandolin had been brought from Amalia's room. She'd showered. Dressed. A footman had delivered a breakfast tray that she'd not touched. There'd been a note from Security informing her when she'd be taken to the airport. She was to remain in her suite until then. Her bedroom, bathroom, lounge—all had views overlooking the sparkling sea. She couldn't see the city—and none of those gathering crowds could see her either.

Her heart beat so hard but she couldn't believe its warning. She couldn't *trust* her feelings.

Surely it was loneliness making her respond so intensely to his attention? He'd trusted her, he'd let her in. It was flattery and infatuation and gratitude. It was the impossibility of anything more. They'd had such a short time to be together of course it was going to feel *perfect*—and as if it would be so for ever. It wouldn't. There would come a point where they didn't want each other this desperately any more. It was just sex. It would pass. The frantic panic of her own pulse was a fraud. Trusting her instincts? No. She couldn't.

Now she wanted the minutes to fly.

Someone knocked on her door and she spun towards it.

'Elsie?' A whisper from behind the wood. 'It's Amalia.'

Elsie sucked in some courage to stabilise her emotions and managed to open the door and smile.

'Have you had breakfast?' Amalia looked at her curiously as she walked in with Callie, the assistant at her side. 'You're very pale.'

'I'm not used to late nights at palace parties.' Elsie tried to joke.

'This is for you, Ms Wynter.' Callie put a large parcel on the writing table and then left.

'From you?' Elsie asked Amalia.

'No.' Amalia shrugged. 'Maybe Felipe?'

Elsie's heart quaked. The parcel was *massive*. She didn't want a gift. She certainly didn't want to open it in front of Amalia. But Felipe wouldn't have sent it with her if it was inappropriate…

'Aren't you going to open it?' Amalia looked intrigued.

She didn't want any kind of recompense for her 'time'. But she couldn't resist tearing the paper. It was a box. And within that box? A custom-made mandolin case. She slowly, reverently opened it. Navy velvet, a gold protective cloth, black silk straps…the colours of Silvabon.

She blinked back tears. How had he got it so *quickly*? She was beyond touched.

'Elsie, it's gorgeous.' Amalia was awed.

'It is.' She put her mandolin into it carefully, taking the time to recover from the explosion of emotion. 'I'm heading to the airport soon.' She made herself speak. 'Before all the crowds line the streets and make it impossible for anyone to move.'

'Don't you want to stay for the coronation? You could stay for longer. Fly later.'

Elsie's heart ached. 'I have to go, Amalia. But I'll email.'

'The ceremony's going to be so boring anyway.'

Elsie looked over at her. 'You're the only family he has who's able to be there.'

Amalia's expression pinched. 'I'm not really family. He wants to send me away.'

'He wants what's best for you.'

'Maybe I want to stay here. But he won't let me.'

Yeah, Elsie had figured that. 'Have you tried telling him how you feel?'

'I don't think he'll listen. He's already decided.'

'Maybe try anyway?' Elsie suggested.

At least she would feel better for having tried.

There was another knock at the door and Callie's voice called for Amalia.

'I'd better get ready,' Amalia said.

'I'm really glad I got to see you again,' Elsie said. 'I'm so sorry I couldn't say goodbye properly last time.'

Amalia nodded and turned but Elsie hurried to the door and pulled the girl into a hug. For a split second Amalia stiffened and Elsie wondered if she'd done the wrong thing. But then Amalia hugged her back, her grip tight.

'Travel safe, Elsie,' Amalia mumbled.

'I will,' Elsie promised. 'And I'll be in touch. I have your personal email now.'

Amalia chuckled. But Elsie meant it. She wasn't letting Amalia down again. Even though she'd end up hearing about Felipe and that would hurt. But she could never avoid all news about him and Amalia was too important.

Moments later, alone again, she touched the mandolin case with trembling fingers. It was so precious, so thoughtful of him. And it said everything, didn't it? How special *he* was. *All* those emotions flooded her.

Could only one day change everything? Could it change her?

One *moment* could change everything. One moment could mean life, or death. Bigger things happened in less time. Trusting this? Trusting her own instincts? Believing in what she felt? She owed herself that. She owed him too. She had to do the right thing. For herself and for him. Which meant she had to take her own advice and *try telling him*.

She had to speak the truth and not hold back. Holding back meant misunderstandings and loneliness. At the very least he would know and she would've released it from her own hold. Keeping secrets. Staying silent for fear of rejection? She was so over that. Saying what she needed to say *mattered*—there was freedom in that even if rejection was inevitable. She would process the emotion eventually, but not if she didn't recognise it, acknowledge it, appreciate it. She had nothing else to lose and she wanted to gift it to him. She wanted *him* to know *he* was loved.

But it was too late. She was stuck in her suite in his palace. Their time had passed. She couldn't break into his private wing.

She would never see him again.

CHAPTER FOURTEEN

Saturday, 11.01 a.m.

IT WAS LESS than an hour until the coronation procession and Felipe needed a smack in the head to pull back his focus. *Do not think about Elsie.* He'd showered, shaved, and dressed entirely on automatic. *Do not dream about Elsie.* He had to concentrate on his country and he was finally almost ready. *Do not ache for Elsie.*

'Sir—'

'I said I didn't want to be interrupted.' He turned to glare at the man who'd walked in unannounced. But Garcia was grey and sweating.

Felipe's blood chilled. 'What is it?'

He held out his hand for the tablet Garcia was holding. It took two seconds to scan the headline and a summary of 'facts'.

Fraudster family breaches palace.

Acid burned the back of his throat. He didn't want her reading this rubbish.

'Someone noticed her last night,' Garcia muttered nervously.

The article shifted the focus from the coronation to his vulnerable stepsister. To Elsie. The threat of something this salacious overshadowing the coronation? His grandfather would be rolling in the family crypt. But his grandfather was dead. And Elsie?

Everything she'd not wanted had been dug up and it would destroy her.

He had done this. By not staying away—not curbing his urges—he'd failed to protect *both* Amalia and Elsie. And how did he recover this now? There was no stopping what people would say. They could only shield themselves—try not to read it? Run away from it?

Impossible.

Rage gripped him. He never should have touched her. Never invited her into his private chambers. She should never have to pay the price for his greed.

'They haven't published it yet,' Garcia said. 'They're asking for exclusive comment before they do.'

Protocol was never to comment on media stories—to 'rise above it', to pretend it wasn't happening. Like the mystery of his father's disappearance.

Don't explain. Suppress emotion. Curiosity will die and we will all carry on.

But it didn't die.

King Javier had insisted it would all be smoothed over by a single abdication announcement weeks after the fact. No one had fronted to answer questions… Only the questions hadn't eased, they had been rehashed every day for weeks until finally his grandfather had fed them Felipe's investiture. Creating a great 'celebration of a new heir!' Seventeen and alone, Felipe had walked into the cathedral in front of his entire country...

But he'd been okay. He'd had the protection of the palace walls. He'd had the sea to dive deep into. And of course there were times when it was hard but he loved his place here.

But his father had only been okay because he'd gone to live a quiet life in Canada where he hadn't seen the drama mentioned every few months in the Silvabon press. His mother, too, had gone—to a quiet existence on an outer island. And the judgement had never really gone away. It never would.

Felipe refused to let anyone else become the target. He hoped to ensure Amalia would be okay by getting her to a secluded school. But Elsie?

If she escaped the country quickly they might not be able to track her down. Which meant they needed to bring her departure forward. She couldn't wait for that flight this afternoon. She certainly couldn't travel with all those people if this story had broken—they'd stare, harass, worse. Feeling afraid? Being judged? This was her nightmare. Her life would be wrecked again, this time because of him. He had to buy her time. Then he'd come up with a decoy. He had no idea what yet, but he'd think of something.

'Tell them if they print it I'll sue,' he said roughly.

'Pardon?'

'Threaten them. They'll hold it at least until we get her out of here.'

He scrolled down past the first paragraph. There was a video embedded in the article. He didn't have to click on it—it played automatically.

Stop watching.

He couldn't. Even as guilt swallowed him.

She asked you not to watch.

He couldn't stop. His eyes stung and his heart raced. Her hair was in a ponytail and she was in jeans and a tee. She looked achingly familiar. Just younger. Sadder. Her husky voice broke his heart. It would break any one *human's* heart. The look shared between mother and daughter? It was so intimate, so deeply personal.

He closed his eyes. But he still saw it—burned in his brain. Such a private moment that should never have been made public.

He knew she had strength now. She'd been forged in fire. But that sweet, vulnerable woman was still inside. She *cared*, despite her determined armour. It was only a thin covering. That was why she didn't stick around, right? Because she could be pierced too easily.

She'd been recorded unknowingly—by someone she trusted invading her privacy. Taking the preciousness of that memory, taking advantage of her for monetary gain. And the dark side of that exposure? Elsie had been turned on by everyone, including her family. The absolute isolation she'd suffered… And that was when he read some of the comments that had been posted online. The shredding of her music, her voice, her very being.

The bitterest bile rose. He couldn't let it happen again.

He utterly understood the loss of privacy, the invasion of deeply personal moments and he felt sharp-edged resignation as they were put forward for public consumption. Funerals. Weddings. Coronations. Even a simple walk around a park or a visit to a café… He intimately knew how it felt to have such private moments put on display and he was always guarded to ensure his deepest feelings remained known only to himself. To protect himself from things like this.

But this had been so much worse than that. This had been a deeply personal moment between a dying mother and her daughter that never should have been witnessed by anyone let alone stolen. Used. And then *scorned*.

So unfairly. So unjustly.

So she shouldn't have to bear the scrutiny and judgement of this damned article now. She shouldn't have her family's past raked over, repeatedly. And it would be repeatedly. Once her name was publicly linked with his, anyone who'd met her in their travels would now sell their stories. It would also be relentless. The exposure was too much for anyone but those hardened to it. Who had the skills to handle it.

That wasn't her. She moved on as soon as the whispers began—choosing fresh start after fresh start.

He couldn't blame her for that. His mother had been miserable in public life. His father had simply run away from it. Felipe had to do better for Amalia and heaven knew he was trying. But he'd made a promise to his grandfather. He needed to be the one who stayed and stood fast.

But he needed to get Elsie far away so she would be safe and free. She should have security and love—a family of her own. Children? He was never bringing children into the palace. He couldn't protect them.

He had to fix this. Because he couldn't stand to watch her wither beneath the glare of those cameras and phones. He had to get her out. He had to see her himself and ensure she understood the urgency.

He brushed past Garcia. 'I'll be back—'

'But, sir—'

He glanced at his watch. Had she left already?

CHAPTER FIFTEEN

Saturday, 11.06 a.m.

SEEKING ONLY ONE THING, Felipe swept past the guards, through the guest wing, straight to Elsie's suite. He opened the door without knocking and slammed it behind him. She was there and he was so relieved he had to put his hand on the wall to brace himself.

'Felipe?' Elsie stifled a scream of surprise.

She was wearing the white and blue billowy dress from that day at the café months ago. Demure yet sexy with that scooped neckline that drew his eye to her lovely neck. Her hair was swept into a messy topknot. Those chunky boots gave her an extra inch in height but not enough for her to be able to look him directly in the eye. That didn't stop her trying.

'You shouldn't be here.' A frantic whisper. 'This is the guest wing. Other people might see you.'

He didn't answer. He couldn't even remember to count to calm down.

'I was getting ready to leave.' Her chest rose and fell as she stared at him. 'Look at you...'

Her gaze brushed over his body. He felt it as if her fingers really were fluttering over his skin. He'd forgotten he was in his uniform—all gold buttons and braid and starch. He stalked towards her—unable to maintain his distance, unable to deny the urge to reach for her and pull her close to ease the ache. Oh, God, he was sorry. He was so, so sorry.

But she stepped to the side. 'Did you do this?' She gestured to the mandolin case open on the writing table behind her. Her voice was husky and sweet and she smiled at him tremulously.

His thundering heart raced faster and faster. Because that look?

Her eyes shimmered with emotion. 'You got a new case so I don't have to strap my old one together every time I want to go somewhere.' She touched the velvet lining gently. 'How did you get the right size so quickly? It's an old instrument—most modern cases aren't the right size.'

'I ordered it a while back.' His voice barely worked.

She blinked. 'A while back?'

'That night you came to the palace.'

'That night?' She licked her lips as if they were parched. 'You ordered this *after* you'd told me to leave?'

'I didn't want you to leave for good.' Not then. His shoulders lifted and he moved to stand beside her. 'I don't want you awkwardly lugging it round in a broken case. It's precious to you and needs better protection.'

Her fingers curled in the soft cloth used to wrap the instrument in. 'How did you get the right size?'

'While we were at dinner—I got my man to measure up.'

'And had it made specially.' Her eyes glistened. 'That was really thoughtful.'

'So this is a gift you can accept?' Unlike the bracelet that was still in his pocket.

'It's the nicest thing anyone's done for me in a really long time,' she said softly.

Silence fell. He knew she was wondering why he was here. He didn't want to tell her. He didn't want to see her expression change. He liked her like this, beautiful and glowing, and he couldn't bear to move.

'You should go.' She cupped his cheek.

He drew a breath in shock and caught the lingering scent of his oil on her skin. His temperature skyrocketed.

'You should be on the way to the procession already.' She swallowed.

He grabbed her wrist, holding her palm to his jaw. 'I'm fully aware of what I should do. It's just that I don't want to do it.'

She gazed into his soul, emotional but unwavering. 'What do you want to do, then?'

Elsie waited for his response, but he was too silent, too rigid—which meant something was wrong.

He was in full regalia for the coronation. The navy fabric hugged his powerful thighs while the braid emphasised his broad shoulders. He looked as if he'd stepped out of a poem from the past—a glorious, vital, virile king. In his prime—powerful and intense, he'd let nothing stand in the way of what he wanted.

'Your Majesty?' She dared him. She couldn't resist.

He wrapped an arm around her waist and she was trapped between him and the table. She read agony in his eyes, but as he slid his other hand beneath the hem of her dress she widened her legs. A growl emerged as he skated a fingertip across her panties.

'You're ready for me,' he muttered.

'From the moment you walked in.' She wanted the wildness. She wanted to soothe the man constrained inside that uniform. She wanted to embrace the feeling he had for her.

It took a mere moment to unzip him. For him to step forward. He gazed into her eyes.

'Take pleasure from me, Felipe.' She tossed his words at him.

The permission he'd once given, she gave back to him. And he took it. Took her. Right there, upright against the table. She hooked her leg around his, her arms around his shoulders, and clung as he thrust.

'Don't let go of me,' she begged, barely balanced in his arms. 'Don't let go.'

His mouth was hers—hard and passionate—his possession complete and unbridled. He locked into her, driving closer and closer and she went soft—

so willing. In seconds his passion sent her over the edge and he cried out in feral agony as he followed.

Shockingly hard. Shockingly quick. Shockingly over.

His hands bit her waist. He ensured her feet had found the floor then stepped back. Her dress dropped into place.

'Elsie…' He was pale and she saw his fingers trembled as he fixed his trousers. There was such regret in his tone.

Both dressed. Both undone.

Felipe couldn't look at her as his brain came back online and his horror grew. 'I apologise.'

He did not lose it like that. Ever. He did not put his entire future at risk. Or *hers*.

'That shouldn't have happened.' He cleared his throat.

None of this should have happened. He couldn't even blame alcohol or a hangover—he hadn't touched anything all evening save three mouthfuls of champagne at last night's dinner. Utterly sober, he'd been drunk on desire, on desperation. High on the heat of her. He'd been so dutiful his entire life and suddenly he'd been so damned out of control.

He swore. 'I didn't use protection. I'm so sorry.'

He loathed himself that second.

She watched him warily. 'Don't worry about that, I'm on the pill. It's easier when I'm travelling.' She swallowed. 'You haven't just got me pregnant.'

He stared at her, trying to process what had just

happened, what she'd just said. His horror deepened as he realised he was feeling a flicker of *disappointment*. Because if there had been a chance of her being pregnant he could have stopped her from leaving. She would've had to stay. Only until she'd seen a doctor. But then he could have stopped her from seeing a doctor...

The escalating thoughts horrified him. The train of imaginings—of *making* her stay? That wasn't just selfish and controlling, it would be ruthless and *insane*. The absolute spoilt whim of a dictator used to getting everything he wanted. Everything his own way—like his grandfather after all.

'It still shouldn't have happened,' he said hoarsely. Because he hadn't known she was covered. He'd gone ahead and taken the risk—without even thinking about it. Without giving a damn.

'Don't regret it.' Her eyes flashed. 'Please don't say that was a mistake.'

'It was.' He swallowed.

Heaven help him, he wanted it again. He wanted to pull her into his arms and rest against her. He wanted to turn his back on the world and forget about everything else in his damned life. So right now he *was* his father. So selfish he'd ignore all other responsibility. When right now, just beyond these palace walls, crowds of people were depending on him, waiting for him. How could he want to forget them all and give everything up just for a woman? For sex. For the best ride of his life.

It was so *weak*. He'd be betraying his country. Breaking the word he'd given to his grandfather. Becoming everything he'd vowed he'd never be…

He *wouldn't*. He couldn't. 'This whole thing was a mistake.'

Elsie paled, her anger obviously mounting. He didn't blame her. She should be angry with him. He was angry with himself. That he'd been momentarily tempted to do *everything* wrong to keep her with him? To cheat and lie and do whatever it took? He loathed the man he could devolve into. Out of control. Selfish. Possessive. Utterly uncaring of everything else. And she would become so miserable.

He could never let it happen.

CHAPTER SIXTEEN

Saturday, 11.18 a.m.

OVERTIRED, OVER-EXPOSED, over-stimulated and overwhelmed by *everything*, Elsie stared. Her eyes were scratchy and dry, her skin felt flayed, while her heart felt as if it had been whipped until raw and bleeding. She'd seen the flash before he'd turned away. She was struggling to recover from that intensity and the fall from ecstasy couldn't have been more sharp or more sudden.

Now he stood with his back to her, his head bowed, and he was walking already. 'I have to leave.'

Without another word? Without even *facing* her?

'What *was* that, Felipe?' she called as he reached the door.

His shoulders straightened. 'I'm sorry. I shouldn't have taken advantage of you.'

He thought he'd taken advantage of her? As if she hadn't been involved, hadn't been *taking* every bit as much as he had? As if she hadn't been *giving*?

'I've never let you take advantage of me,' she said proudly. 'I've taken what I wanted. What did you want? Why did you just come in here?' she asked. 'Was it for one last quickie? To take the edge off before your big show? Is that what this was?'

He turned, his back to the door, anger reeking from his rigid stance. 'I came to tell you—' He inhaled sharply. 'My private jet is ready. It has clearance to leave as soon as you're onboard.'

She stilled. 'You want me to leave now?'

'Yes.'

'Not on the commercial flight later? Not after your coronation? Now?'

'Now. Yes.'

'What about all the other royals and their security? Isn't this problematic?'

Why was he so desperate to get rid of her that he was bending all the damn rules?

'Not at all,' he clipped.

So she could request a flyover of the damn cathedral in which his coronation would be happening—make such a noise he couldn't ignore her? Why wait for some jet when she could do *that* now?

Because what those last few minutes had proven more than anything, was how human he was. How deeply he too needed connection. Needed love. Of *course* she'd fallen in love with him. He wasn't perfect. He was as flawed as she, in as much need of play, laughter and love. She needed to be honest with him. And now she had her chance.

'No.'

'No?' He stared at her. 'What do you mean no?'

'Not used to hearing that word, are you?' She tried to smile but failed. 'You try not to be, but you're still spoilt in some ways, Felipe. You still expect to get whatever you want, whenever you want.'

He paled. 'I just said I was sorry—'

'I'm not talking about what just happened. I wanted that too. We both know that,' she interrupted. 'I'm talking about the rest of your damned life.'

He stared at her.

'You've carved out time in these last twenty-four hours. They should have been the busiest yet, but you got yourself out of it. Meetings with advisers that you blew off? You did that to see *me*. Why can't you do that the rest of the time? Your life doesn't have to be completely conscripted. You could have the time and space for a personal life. I think you *choose* not to because it's *easier* for you not to.'

'Easier?' A scoffing snort.

'Putting yourself first sometimes isn't a crime, Felipe. You're allowed to want things for yourself. You're allowed to want me. Maybe even for more than one day.'

She bit her lip. She wanted him to more than *want* her. She wanted him to need her, to love her. And she had to speak her own truth.

But he shut down. 'You need to go, Elsie. Now. This is over.'

She summoned all her courage. 'I don't think it is.'

He regarded her solemnly but then his gaze slid from hers and he actually fidgeted.

Warily she watched him. 'What aren't you telling me?'

'Someone at the dinner last night must have tipped off the press. I've seen an article they want to publish. They've done their digging.'

'About me.'

He nodded curtly. 'I've managed to delay its release. You can get safely away from here before it lands.'

She braced against her instinctive shudder. She could handle this. 'It doesn't matter.' She squared her shoulders. 'I've been through it before. There's actually *nothing* worse than what I've already been through.'

His jaw tensed. 'You don't understand. You can't handle what they're going to throw at you, Elsie. Whatever online hate you had before, it'll be nothing on this.'

'You're underestimating me. You, the one person I thought actually gave me a chance, now think I'm not up to it?'

'I don't want you to be hurt,' he said grimly.

'It's not any media that will hurt me, Felipe. Real hurt is far more personal than that.'

He stiffened. '*This* isn't real,' he said. 'This will never be real, Elsie.'

He was shutting them down before they had the chance to really explore it.

'Not if you remain so completely closed to the possibility that it *could* be more,' she argued. 'You'd decided that from the start. I'm just your convenient distraction, a final fling in the countdown to the all-important coronation.'

'Is that so awful? Is it so wrong to have something fun for myself?' he asked. 'You're the one who just said I needed that. And *you* said yes. You agreed it could only be this one night.'

'So I did. Now I'm just telling you the rest of the truth. You don't want *me* to be hurt? *You* don't want to hurt anyone? Too bad. Life doesn't work like that. We all hurt people. Especially those we care about. Making mistakes is part of being human.'

'So you finally agree this has been a mistake?'

'Never. I will never regret this.'

'Even though I used you.'

She reeled at the sudden flex. 'Don't cheapen what's happened between us.'

'Sex, Elsie. What's happened is a lot of *sex*.'

'No.' She would not let him reframe this that way.

'It's been less than a day,' he said shortly. 'Let me assure you, whatever you think you feel, it's *not* real.'

'Are you denying what I have to say? What I feel? Won't you listen?'

'Elsie—'

'You trusted me and believed in me only last night when I told you about my father. You took me at face value months ago, took my word then. But not in *this*?' She frowned at him. Why—what was so different? Her heart ached. 'Wow, so the one thing you can't believe *isn't* the worst of me, it's that I could want more from you?' She stared at him as the truth dawned. 'You don't want to be loved.'

He bristled. 'I have too much else to do to be responsible for keeping you happy.'

She breathed out at the hit—keeping her *happy*? 'You don't have to keep me happy. That's not what letting yourself love me—love anyone—would mean.'

Did he equate all love with duty? As a burden of care and responsibility?

Because he'd spent his life trying to keep people happy. His grandfather. His mother. Now Amalia. He'd carried the burden of other people who had torments, illnesses, griefs of their own. And he didn't want to shoulder any more—because he didn't believe he was enough for any of them. For anyone.

It turned out her spoilt king was the ultimate people-pleaser. And he never really took time to please himself personally.

'You wouldn't have to do any of that for me,' she said. 'All I'd want is to be in your life. To *share* things *with* you—the good and the bad. To be as honest with you as we've been this last night. With truth there's trust, right?'

He was very still. 'There are things you'll want to do in your life that you couldn't do if you stayed here.'

'Maybe but maybe not. I know you're the King, I know there are expectations that you will always meet because you love Silvabon and you love the people here and you love the palace even though you've had heartache here. I would never want you to renounce your duty or your crown.' Her heart raced. 'The thought of a public element to my life scares me a little but I know you'd help me. And maybe I could then even help *you* with it? I could help others too, couldn't I? I could find something…' She trailed off as she saw the tension in his face, but she couldn't stop herself from fighting for him. He was so worth it. 'You don't have to be alone in everything, Felipe. You could have it all—the crown, yes, and a wife, and children. And with us all together, supporting each other, it could be okay…?'

'I've seen people try, remember?' he said harshly, denying her. 'They all fail.'

She stared at him so determinedly standing alone and implacable. 'You're like a rock in the centre of a fast-flowing river. All the water is swirling around but you're always there, always anchoring others. Steadfast and dependable, right? But you need your own strength replenished. You can't keep holding on for everyone else for ever. That's not fair.'

'Life isn't fair.'

'But you don't have to be *alone*. You don't have to sacrifice everything for everyone else. You can have your dreams. Your person. You could have me.' She inhaled shakily and confessed it all. '*I* would love you. I've *already* fallen in love with you. Felipe…'

Felipe stood so still—not hearing, not believing. He had to stop her from talking. From confusing him and making every cell inside him ache for something so much more than physical. He was shaking on the inside and he had to stop her from saying *that*.

'I watched the video,' he muttered harshly.

'You…what?' She stared at him, clearly derailed. *'What?'*

'It's embedded in the article they've written. It played automatically.'

'Why didn't you stop it?'

Because he couldn't breathe. Because she was beautiful. Because once it had started he simply couldn't do anything.

'I asked you not to,' she whispered. 'You said you wouldn't.'

She was truly hurt now. Pinched and pale and shocked. She'd not believed he'd have ever done that. But he had. Maybe he shouldn't have told her, but he couldn't not. He felt too awful not to be honest with her. And now he had to hurt her more. He was being cruel to be kind. He had to push her away. He had to make her run. Because he couldn't cope with what she was saying. Not now. Not ever.

Her eyes shimmered with reproach. 'You broke your promise to me.'

'Yes.' His throat tightened. Never had he regretted anything more.

He'd betrayed her. And now she shut down in front of him. He saw it—the change, the defiance

blooming in her eyes. He leaned against the door—
stopping himself from leaning into her.

'So the thought of this becoming anything
more—' She looked at him directly and asked sadly,
'That's a hard no?'

He couldn't answer that.

'You only had to let me in,' she said. 'Only let me
love you. You only had to be there for me.'

No. That wasn't right. 'You should have so much
more than that, Elsie. You should have someone
love you too. I can't be the man who does. I don't
have—' He shook his head. 'Can't.'

'Won't,' she said brokenly. 'You won't. There's
a difference.'

'Can't.' He couldn't bear to see her wither. People
didn't thrive at the palace.

His mother had faded. His father had run away.
His grandfather had become like stone—unyielding, uncompromising. And suddenly he was furious
with her for not believing him. He'd *seen* it, lived it
and he could *not* see her suffer. She'd want to leave
eventually. And when she did? It would destroy him.
So she had to go now. Before the damage to them
both was irreparable. And he was so angry he could
scarcely see straight.

Only *her* anger propelled her forward. She marched
up to him and planted her feet so she stood right in
front of him. He couldn't escape. He could only push.

'Was I just someone convenient who you wanted
only because you knew you couldn't have me for

long? The thrill of the challenge? The fun of deception and claiming someone completely inappropriate for your status?' Elsie did *not* want to believe that. But she didn't know what to believe now.

He'd seen it. The one person she didn't want to. It was something so private that had been so shredded and he'd *promised*...

And now here he was telling her he needed her to leave. He didn't have the energy for her. She wasn't worth the effort. And the rejection hurt. The denial of her feelings, of her value, sliced so deep, creating a wound like none before. She'd thought he understood her—that they'd understood each other. And now she was angry because, not only was she unwanted, she felt a fool. All over again. She'd had no idea of the ugly truth—just as she'd believed her father had been genuine in that crowdfunding effort when it had been just a scam to get more of what he'd wanted. This was a scam too—Felipe had made her fall with his charm and his assurances. Only he'd lied.

'I thought you were strong, but you don't even know what strong is.' She stepped forward, unable to hold back from blasting her feelings at him. 'Strong is standing up for change. Strong is saying this is me, this is what I want. Strong is taking charge of your own life. Strong is saying no to an impossible pressure. Strong is making personal needs a priority. Strong is accepting people into your life when you've been hurt before.'

Finally she realised the problem. The burden of

the crown was his *excuse* to cut himself off. What he *feared* was people leaving him again. The people he'd loved had left. And he didn't trust anyone to stay. That was why he wouldn't open his heart to anyone. Why he didn't want children. It broke her heart. But made her angry too. He was so terrified of loss he couldn't even *try*.

'And are you so very strong?' he taunted harshly. 'You run away like a wounded animal every time you think someone might think less of you. You don't ride out any storms. You're petrified of rejection. You're the one who won't follow dreams.'

'What am I doing *right now*, Felipe?' she yelled at him. 'Putting myself so far *over* the line. Strong is trying to make change and not giving up even when it's an ongoing struggle. You won't even redecorate your Elizabethan-orgy-style bedroom because you're so constrained by *duty*.'

He sucked in a shocked breath. 'I *cannot* do this right now, Elsie. I have my bloody coronation.'

'You cannot do this *ever*. You *won't*.' She was so hurt by his denial. 'You made me trust you. When you gave me a chance with Amalia, when you believed me when I told you everything. You gave me hope and made me think that maybe…' She paused to pull herself together—and failed. 'But *I'm* not enough for you to get past it completely.'

And that devastated her.

Her only *mistake* had been in thinking there was nothing worse for her to suffer. There was so much worse. Because before it had been the past that had been picked apart. Her choices, her actions—she'd been crucified for them. She'd been rejected—cast out to be alone. But this was the *future*. This was *hope*. He'd given her all of that only to then destroy it. So suddenly, so completely. And she damned him for it.

'I can't be ashamed of my family for the rest of my life,' she said. 'They made such bad choices, but those choices weren't *mine*. I won't suffer that punishment any more. I'm worth someone's trust and *I* can *keep* trust. I'm worth someone's love and I have value to give. It might not be palaces and gold and jewels and an army, but I have other more important things. I have a *heart*. I'm not no one. I'm not nothing.' She stared at him. 'You don't want to *make* someone have to stay with you, but maybe they'd *choose* to. It's the height of arrogance to assume that no one else could understand your world. That no one else could handle it. That you couldn't make the changes necessary if you really wanted to.'

'Elsie—'

'Reject *me*, fine, but don't do that to Amalia. She likes it here. She feels safe here. Talk to her. You managed that for me once, do it for her. She deserves that. Don't send her away.'

'I'm not. She—'

'Have you actually *asked* her whether she wants to go?'

He jerked his head. 'I want her to have her freedom.'

'Freedom is when you *know* you're loved,' she argued. 'That family is there for you. That, no matter what, your people have your back. And that even if you make a mistake, if you're sorry, they'll forgive you if you ask.' She lifted her head. 'I would have forgiven my father, Felipe. My brother. But they didn't want that from me. They didn't want me. They don't love me. I would have forgiven you too—if you'd asked. But you don't want my forgiveness. You're *not* sorry. And you don't want me either.' She got it now. 'So no, thank you, I don't want your damned private jet. I don't want any special treatment. I'm not some *mistake* you can just kick out of your precious country. I am not something to be ashamed of.'

She was so hurt.

'I'm doing this for you—'

'You are *not*. I don't give a damn what they write about me, don't you get that? I've had it all. Worse already. And I survived. I'll survive again. I am so much stronger than you'll ever let yourself believe. But none of that matters because I'm still never going to be good enough for you. *You're* the one who cares what they think.'

'I know how they can destroy you.'

'The only person destroying part of me right now is *you*.' She shook. 'It was never about what everyone else—what *random strangers*—said. It was that the people who I loved…*they* didn't believe in me. They didn't have my back or even try to understand. That's what hurt. And that's *you* now.'

He'd let her down and he didn't care. Because if

he did, he wouldn't have done it. But he really did want her to go.

He closed his eyes briefly. 'I never meant to hurt you.'

She laughed bitterly. 'You think you're so honourable? So dutiful. But in less than a day, you betrayed me. Maybe you did use me. Did you scare yourself, Felipe? Wanting me so badly you risked being unsafe with me? Were you finally vulnerable? Did that frighten you?'

His eyes flashed.

'I'm not the one who has anything to hide, am I?' she realised scornfully. 'Being abandoned hurts. And you won't let anyone close enough again. That's why you're sending Amalia away. And me. You can't risk your own heart. You're not willing to even try. You're a coward.' She was so hurt. 'It's all an excuse, to stop *yourself* being hurt.'

He was shaking too. 'I'm trying to protect *you*.'

'You're protecting yourself. Go right ahead. Be as rigid as your grandfather, as emotionally unavailable as both of your parents. Be an isolated island of a king, Felipe. Be lonely always. Because *I* won't. I've handled so much I'll even get over you.'

'Elsie—'

'I'm not ashamed of anything I've done these last twenty-four hours. Or indeed any of my life. I'm *not* hiding any more. So go and do your damned duty. You—' She broke off and drew breath. 'Leave. *Now.*'

CHAPTER SEVENTEEN

Saturday, 12.01 p.m.

FELIPE WALKED SLOWLY, leading his stallion. His head was bare beneath the burning sun and he was alone for this part of the procession—walking as an unadorned, humble man—to be crowned King. In the cathedral he would be robed, handed a sceptre, an orb, and finally crowned. The throngs of people lining each side of his path were silent, as was custom. The only thing he could hear was the beat inside his head. He counted, keeping it slow, keeping himself calm. It wasn't working. He couldn't focus.

He'd *made* her leave. He'd *lied* to her. When she valued truth so deeply.

I used you.

But he'd protected her—hadn't he? It was all he'd really wanted to do.

He swallowed back bitterness as he recalled her accusations and the deeply buried vat of hurt she'd ripped open. His father had left him. So had his mother. His grandfather had burdened him with so much that *wasn't* personal. He'd emphasised his duty—rules, regulations, requirements. So if he didn't do this now—who would he be then? Who would he be without the crown?

No one. Anyone.

And part of him was tempted. Because he wanted everything he didn't think he could have as long as he had the crown on his head. He wanted *her.*

He had never ever been tempted to walk away from it all. Until now he'd been unable to understand his father. He'd thought it weak that Carlos had abdicated and left in the dead of night. And yes, maybe it wasn't the best way he'd gone about it, but he appreciated now that it had taken his father a courage of his own. Maybe Carlos hadn't been able to figure out a compromise with King Javier... Yeah, compromise hadn't existed in the old man's mind. And the way Amalia's mother had been vilified in the press? Hell, she *still* was even after she'd died, which was why Felipe felt so protective towards Amalia.

Finally Felipe totally understood why Carlos would've wanted to get the woman he loved far away from here. But *here* was also amazing. The media was only one minor element and he *couldn't* let them win. He couldn't stop this walk any more than he could stop breathing. This was his home. His soul. *His* crown. He didn't want to turn his back on his country. But he wanted to keep Elsie close. And safe. And yet she didn't want him to turn his back on his country either—not at *all.*

The temptation of her offer called to him.

I would do anything for you.

The wickedness rose. He wanted her to live in the castle as his concubine. To secretly swim with him every morning and be there in his room for him at night to return to. She could live in a different room every day for three years and still have more to explore. She'd be his secret. It was pure fantasy and it was appalling how tantalising it was.

She could work in the café still, during the day. He'd build another secret tunnel so she could get there. But secrets escaped. And for her to be some secret as if he were ashamed? She'd grow pale and miserable and lonely. He couldn't let that happen. She deserved so much more than that.

She'd been destroyed once. But she'd risen from the ashes like a phoenix, hadn't she? Stunning and strong, beautiful and proud. She'd been so proud when she'd stood in front of him today. Regal in her slaying of his doubts and shattering his defences. She'd believed in him more than he believed in himself. She'd expected more from him. Yet she'd accepted everything.

His failure. His heartache. And hers.

He slowly mounted the steps of the cathedral, aware of the absolute silence of the crowds around him. For so many people to be so quiet and focused?

His entire country was watching, waiting for him. Millions more were watching around the world. He couldn't expect them to wait longer by putting his personal interests ahead of the gift they'd given him in attending the ceremony today. This was about far *more* than him. Now wasn't the time. He would not fail them.

He made his promises, clearly, honestly, meaning every word.

The crown was placed on his head. It was heavy. So was the cloak. And his hands were full with the sceptre and the orb. Everything was real and weighing a tonne. A literal burden. But as music played in celebration? That was when his mind wandered again.

Don't let go of me.

She wanted a home. Someone to *want* her to stay. He remembered her smoky eyes and her excitement at the lightest of restraint plays. She'd wanted him to make it *impossible* for her to leave. She didn't want to be released. She wanted to be *kept*. Not as a possession. Not as a thing. But safe and secure.

Maybe she'd wanted to be held because she'd been afraid of asking him if she could stay. But in the end she *had* asked. She'd opened up and told him how she felt. She'd been vulnerable and brave in admitting that she wanted to be a permanent, living fixture in his heart.

Which was exactly where she was already.

Only he hadn't told her. He hadn't realised—until right now. Right now when he was in front of millions and unbearably lonely without her. He wanted her *beside* him. Not watching from the palace. Not waiting in some secret chamber. But walking *alongside* him. He would be so proud to have her with him. And he didn't want to do it without her. And he didn't give a damn what anyone would have to say about it. Somehow he would shut down any rogue reporting. Or maybe he would just rise above it with her. Because being with her gave his heart wings.

But would she stay here in Silvabon?

Have you actually asked her?

Elsie had been referring to Amalia. And he hadn't asked her either. He'd made a unilateral decision— as if he knew best. An autocratic dictator. His grandfather all over—trying to do what was best, yes, but not understanding everything. It was so much more nuanced than that. He'd been such a fool. Because yes, he'd been afraid.

He had to ask Elsie. He'd never asked her. He should have given her the *choice*. But she needed to know his feelings first and right now he had to let her go. There wasn't time. Too many people were counting on him to be here *now*. She was counting on him too. Not to betray her to the public. Not to turn that spotlight on her. Not without even the limited protections he could put in place first. They needed time alone and that was hardly about to happen. But he'd let her believe he didn't care. He'd let her think *he* didn't believe her. He'd belittled her feelings. And he couldn't let that stand. He had to tell her how he felt.

He could envisage it. He'd get to the airport. Halt her plane. Board it if she had already. Otherwise he'd corner her in the terminal. He could make a public declaration—an invitation, a proposal. But it would be one she wouldn't want because she wouldn't be able to answer with complete honesty. Not with the world watching. And they would be. Everything was up for consumption. Weddings. Funerals. Coronations. Dates. Proposals. All picked over and commented upon. The lack of privacy was insufferable—even that balcony in his own damned bedroom was a relic of public consumption from years gone by and all that had happened since was that the audience was even bigger. Everything personal could be live-streamed to anyone who bothered to click the link and he refused to have what was between them shared to anyone. It was too precious.

But if he let her go now, if she got on that plane without him stopping her, she wouldn't come back. She'd made her stand. She'd offered everything he'd wanted and he'd rejected her. She wouldn't return to make the offer again. She was too hurt. Which meant he couldn't let her go without telling her how he really felt. And how did that happen away from this audience of millions?

There wasn't any time. Not now. He had to be here for his people. He'd never let them down. He would do this properly—to the very best that he could. So he didn't mount his horse as he was supposed to. He gestured to his waiting groom to hold for a moment and stepped forward alone, deciding on an impromptu walkabout. He saw Garcia's fierce look but ignored it. These people had been waiting for hours to get a glimpse of him and to be part of these celebrations. He walked towards the crowd. They were not silent now. They'd swiftly settled in a chant.

'Felipe! Felipe! Felipe!'

He could imagine Elsie teasing him about the size of his head. He smiled at the thought and the cheering crescendoed to deafening decibel levels. Hell, he wished she were with him. Because he loved Silvabon. The people. The palace. The city, sea, sky. He would give *anything* in his country's best interests. It had his heart completely. But so did she. And it was only now that he realised his heart was so much bigger than he'd ever known. It could hold it *all*—most especially her.

'Thank you.' He bowed to the group of people nearest the railing. Their cameras flashed but their smiles were brighter.

'You're the King.'

'Yes.'

He didn't often talk to children but this one was being held up by her father. And Felipe couldn't help thinking of that shocking dismay from earlier when Elsie had said he couldn't have just got her pregnant. Both the disappointment and the desire still lingered. He'd sworn he wasn't going to have children—that he didn't want them to be heirs to all that was the Crown. But Elsie had called him out on that too, hadn't she? He could alter the weight of it. He could build in choices. He'd been too wary— too rigid—to give that full consideration before. But now? Now he ached for *everything*— especially children. *Her* children. The laughter he could imagine…the footsteps…the music.

'Where's your queen?' The little girl gave him a smile.

'I don't have one yet,' he said huskily.

'Can I be the Queen?'

A ripple of laughter went around the surrounding crowd.

'Unfortunately not at this time,' he informed her gravely.

'Is it because I'm not a princess?'

'No, I think anyone can be a queen' he replied. 'But you're a little young.'

The little girl frowned, apparently considering his words. 'You need to find someone else. You'd better hurry up.'

Out of the mouths of babes. 'You're right. I'll see what I can do.'

With a smile at her parents, he stepped back and signalled to his groom. A moment later he swung up onto his horse.

As the crowd cheered, he saluted them. This was good for Silvabon. For the promotion of alliances, for tourism. But his heart still ached. He did need his Queen.

He made himself maintain the slow trot and not gallop back to the palace as if he were racing for the moon. He smiled, occasionally waved, nodded in appreciation of their attention. He'd been rehearsing for this moment all his life. He knew exactly what to do. And he wanted to do it. It felt right.

He would be their king. But he would also be a

man. And men made mistakes. Men weren't perfect. Sometimes they had to be strong and face their fears. And ask for forgiveness.

Back inside the palace, he strode through the private wing. He hardly had any time.

'Is everything okay?' Amalia asked as he swept past her. 'You look pale.'

'I need to make a call.' But he hurriedly swivelled back to face her. 'You know, you don't have to go to boarding school if you don't want to.'

She stared at him.

'You can go to a local school here in Silvabon. Live in the palace. We can get additional music tutors. Or you could go to summer camps for music or something…' He watched the colour wash into her face. 'I thought you'd hate it here, but if you don't.' He cleared his throat. 'If you'd rather stay…' He drew a breath and realised another powerful truth. 'I'd like you to stay.'

She stared at him for a moment.

'That's if—'

'I want to stay,' she said quickly. 'I want to go to school here.'

'Really?' Relief then a small bit of happiness hit—maybe he could have a little family. But he wanted so much more. He wanted *Elsie*. 'Okay. Talk more later.'

Amalia nodded. 'Thank you, Felipe.' Her smile was shy.

As if he were a kind and benevolent king? He shook his head. 'I should have asked what you wanted sooner. I'm sorry.' He glanced at his watch and his heart stopped.

'Are you sure you're okay?' Amalia asked.

'Yeah.' He flashed his sister an appreciative smile and hoped like hell he would be.

Adrenalin flowed in his veins and he ran up the stairs three at a time. He knew what he needed to do. And he needed to do it *now*.

'It's time for the balcony appearance.' His aide was reading his tablet as he walked into the ante-chamber. 'The flyover is four minutes out.'

'No. I need a brief break.'

'Sir?' His aide froze. Only his eyeballs swivelled, giving a side-eye that would've been funny if Felipe weren't so frantic.

Elsie's flight couldn't leave until after the flyover. Which meant he had only minutes to contact her. Four minutes wasn't going to be enough. 'I need to make a phone call. Stall the flyover. Give me a phone.'

He hadn't had one on him for the ceremony. This action was so unsophisticated. So simple. So desperate. But it was all he could think to do.

'Sir, we *can't*.' The poor aide was having conniptions.

'We can and we will. Adapt and get used to it.' He shot the guy a twisted smile. 'Some things are going to have to change.'

CHAPTER EIGHTEEN

Saturday, 03.38 p.m.

'WE HAVE TO wait for the flyover, then you'll be able to board the plane.'

Elsie nodded as Captain Ortiz reminded her of the plan. No one else in the waiting lounge seemed to mind the delay but it was sending Elsie's blood pressure to the stratosphere. Everywhere she turned there was another screen. There'd been no avoiding any of the coronation—from the procession to the cathedral, to the service inside, to the procession back to the palace again. Everyone wanted to watch the entire thing. Weren't they tired of staring at him? Apparently not.

She'd been driven in a car as part of the guest procession as he'd planned. They'd gone across the palace esplanade, towards the cathedral in the centre of the city. Then they'd taken a left when everyone else continued straight ahead. Under cover of a bridge there'd been a rendezvous and a change of car. Again with fully tinted windows. Felipe hadn't been joking when he'd told her his security team was intense. But maybe they'd been right to be. The streets had been lined with citizens. Most were dressed in the country's colours—that deep navy and gold. They were all bright smiles. The hum of excitement breached the bulletproof glass and low rumble of her car. They loved their king. His honour and duty to his country was appreciated. He was a good guy. Spoilt, yes. But still good. But right now she wanted to hate him.

Even though he'd believed in her, that he knew she did the right thing, he didn't want her. He didn't want to fight or make an effort for her or make whatever changes might need to happen. *She* was lacking and unlovable in some way. And while that hurt, she had to believe that he was using her own vulnerability as a convenient excuse as well. In truth *no* woman was ever going to be good enough for him. She felt sorry for that gorgeous betrothal princess who he'd refused. That *she* wasn't good enough? It was an impossible pedestal to mount and he didn't want to put any woman up for that kind of scrutiny.

But more than that, he didn't believe *he* was good enough. That was why he wouldn't fight. His mother had been devastated by the very public break-up of her marriage. His father hadn't been able to cope with the pressures of palace life and had left with his lover. Now Felipe was trying to protect Amália from feeling the same by sending her away from it for periods of time. And he? He'd built such defences he wouldn't let anyone in. He wouldn't let anyone *stay*.

Predictably, Ortiz hadn't just dropped her at the airport. Apparently he'd been assigned as a protection officer for her. But she knew he was Felipe's main protection, which meant he wasn't doing the job he was meant to on this most important public and presumably most risky of days.

'You should be with the King,' she said.

'I'm where His Majesty needs me to be.'

She knew there were other guards watching her from a greater distance. It was so unnecessary. Even if that media story was going to run it wouldn't be until after the coronation. So she shouldn't be the priority today. 'Are you going to board the plane with me?'

'Yes.'

She was surprised. 'How long are you going to be guarding me?'

'My next orders will come through once we land.'

A wave of misery hit. She didn't want that. She needed to be free of him to heal. The possibility of drawn-out links to Felipe gave her false hope that he wanted to ensure more than her safety. Maybe he wanted to know where she was? Maybe he would come after her?

She shivered. Dreams like those were self-destructive. She needed to end it completely and she would once she'd landed elsewhere. She just needed to get through the last of this day.

She'd picked a chair that faced away from the giant TV screen but had still been able to hear the nauseating official commentary.

'He's paused at the top of the stairs. His head

bowed. The weight of a nation on his shoulders, the eyes of the world upon him right now...'

But it had been the endlessly pro-Felipe indulgent opinions of the other plane passengers that had destroyed her thin emotional control.

'He looks very alone. Why wouldn't his mother come to the coronation?'

'She's never returned to the palace since Prince Carlos left her, isn't that awful?'

'She left Felipe alone with King Javier?'

Yeah. No wonder Felipe was so defensive of his heart. His mother couldn't overcome her own hurt or grief to be there for her son and Elsie knew he'd tried to reach out to her. But his mother hadn't seen that he could have used her support as well as offering her his. His father hadn't been able to face the burden of the Crown and the judgement against his lover. They'd both abandoned him to face everything alone. Elsie couldn't blame him if he was angry with his parents for that. If he was wary of others doing the same.

'That's Princess Sofia of Charlemeux. I don't think she's right for him.'

Elsie had shrivelled inwardly as the cameras had panned through the audience pointing out all those presidents, princes, princesses to the millions watching on the live stream. Amalia was in the front row. There had been a rippling murmur of support for the way he'd become guardian to his stepsister.

'It's not her fault her mother was such a—'

At that point Elsie had resorted to staring at the floor. She'd wished her headphones weren't lost somewhere in the bottom of her bag. Her original plan had been to go to Madrid, find work, carry on as usual. Only she didn't want the usual few months here, months there any more. She was *tired*. She didn't want to be moving all the time. She wanted a permanent home. She wanted to build a career, build a network of friends, maybe even build herself a family one day. She'd go home to England. She'd have her own café. She'd have a quiet, fulfilling life. She'd be okay.

That news about her being in the palace might break but news would blow over. It had before. And that news—that *notoriety*—wasn't the true cause of her heartache.

She'd watched him walk back down that long aisle, the crown heavy, the sword at his side, the sceptre and orb in his hands and she'd still felt a flicker of pride for him. Strong and dutiful. He'd been a lone figure in front of his soldiers but he'd done what he was born to do. Now he had another celebratory dinner ahead of him. More fireworks. He was caught fast in his world and all she could hope was that one day he'd meet a woman who'd love him the way he ought to be loved. Just for himself. Someone who he loved enough to lower his barriers. Someone who would play with him, with whom he could laugh and laze about within those rare moments he allowed. She wanted him to be happy.

But yeah, right now she still hated him. She hated how much she felt for him.

'How much longer until that flyover?' she asked Ortiz anxiously.

'Apologies Ms Wynter.' Ortiz looked tense as he glanced at his watch. 'It should be any moment. But it will take a few minutes, I'm sorry.'

She really didn't want his pity.

'You missed a great tour this morning.'

She turned at the voice. It was the man who'd sat across the aisle from her on the flight in.

'It was a real treat,' he added. 'I'm going to bring my wife here for our next holiday.'

She smiled. 'That's great.'

Whereas she was never, *ever* coming back here.

'Ms Wynter?'

She turned. Ortiz was looking ridiculously expressionless, which *really* made her worry.

'Is something wrong?' She stepped nearer.

'I have a call for you.'

She realised he was holding a phone to his chest.

'If you'll follow me, there's a private room.'

She remembered what had happened the last time she'd followed this guy—abduction to the palace. Her heart thundered. But this time Ortiz really did lead her to a nearby room and then left her in there alone with that phone.

'Hello?'

'Elsie.' Felipe, sounding rough and rushed. 'We need to talk.'

Her legs hollowed out but she paced around the small room. 'You're supposed to be stepping onto the palace balcony overlooking the esplanade right now. The whole world is waiting.'

'They can wait another couple of minutes.'

'You're holding up a plane full of people too. We can't board until after the flyby.'

'The flyby won't happen until this call ends. So it's your choice, Elsie.'

Her choice? She stilled.

'You can get on that plane or you could come back to the palace so we can speak,' he explained. 'But know this: if you get on the plane, I will follow. As soon as the formalities are over here, I'll come to you. The world will know and there'll be drama and all that if you want.'

She really didn't want that. But she wanted him. She yearned for him. And all she could do was grip the phone more tightly and listen.

'Or...' He drew an audible breath. 'You can get back into the car with Ortiz and come back to the palace so we can talk face to face as soon as this show is over.'

'We don't have anything to talk about, Felipe.'

'There's something I need to tell you.' His voice caught.

Her heart ached as she heard the break in him. 'You can't tell me now?'

'Elsie…'

She closed her eyes because suddenly hope soared and she couldn't handle it. 'Don't do this, Felipe.'

'Don't leave, Elsie.' The softest breath. 'Please don't leave me.'

At the precise moment every citizen and guest in Silvabon was looking skyward, King Felipe was looking in the middle distance. He was beyond tense and couldn't even count. Then he caught it—the slow progression of a sleek black car through the back streets where the crowds weren't gathered. It made its way towards the tunnel that would take it to the palace's underground entrance. Another ten minutes and she would be within the room.

He lifted his gaze and finally breathed. The aerial display was impressive. Their pilots were few in number but elite in skill. Streams of colour flowed from the planes—the navy and gold of Silvabon. He raised his hand. Braved a smile.

The fact was he was more nervous than he'd never been in his life.

Ten minutes later he swept along the corridor. He'd inwardly debated where he'd wanted Ortiz to bring her. His bedroom was the first place that sprang to mind. Then the cave. Neither were appropriate. They needed privacy but she also needed to know she wasn't a prisoner. That was him.

He'd settled on his private library. No guests would see her and the windows gave the room a light and airy feel and she'd not been in there. They had no history in that room.

She was already there, still wearing the blue and white, sweet and sexy dress. Her face was pale and her gaze wide and his heart stopped. It took everything not to take her into his arms and dispense with words altogether. But she needed words. He needed to figure them out.

'I'm sorry.' Simple. True.

She was so still.

He took a step forward. Then stopped.

'Do you know what I want?' He shook his head, starting the wrong way already. 'You said I was spoilt. I'm *worse* than spoilt. I'm possessive and selfish. I want you for me. You're mine. No one else's. Not even Amalia's. I want you in my bed, waiting for me. My secret pleasure. I don't want to share you at all. And I don't ever want this—' he gestured around the room and all its gilded features '—to change what we have. It changed my mother. My father. Amalia even maybe. It changes everyone. Never for the better. I don't want *this*, this joy between us, to end. Ever.'

Her whole body shook. 'This joy?' A whisper, an echo.

His heart burst and his secrets spilled. 'So I have this fantasy about keeping you in the palace in secret. But I can't. You deserve so much more than that. I didn't want kids because I thought I shouldn't and then today I'm desperate to hold onto you and

I forget…and then I imagine your children—*our* children—and suddenly I've never wanted anything more and I want to change things up all differently so we can keep them safe and happy and free and I don't know who I am any more,' he growled. 'And it terrifies me. And what you said to me earlier? I couldn't listen. I couldn't *stand* to listen.'

And he couldn't stand now because he was tired—tired of fighting it, tired of holding back, tired of being strong, of being afraid. He was so damn tired he sank right where he was. And then he was just a man on his knees—all but hopeless as he tried to make her understand the things he could hardly make sense of himself.

'But at the same time it's the only thing I want to hear,' he mumbled. 'And I want to hear it again and again because it will never be enough.' The yawning void in him couldn't ever be filled and how had he handled the delight of her? By pushing her away. He was the master of his own devastation and he was furious with himself. 'I lied to you. And I hurt you and I am so sorry. And too late I realised that what terrifies me more than anything is the thought of you leaving me. I don't want you to leave me. Ever. So if you stay, know that I couldn't…that for me it's for ever. That's what I want. For ever. With you.'

Helpless, he watched a tear trickle down her cheek and his own throat choked up.

'You just appeared and you lit everything up,' he admitted, so sad to see her so upset. 'You made me laugh. You make me want to play. You gave me a sense of freedom to the point that I didn't care about the crown and that scares me too.'

Everything scared him. But mostly this. Mostly seeing her pale and silent and wiping away her tears. But then she moved. She walked towards him.

'Of course you still care about it.' Compassion shone from those blue eyes and he really didn't deserve it. 'You just stood through three hours of pomp and ceremony. You can be both things, Felipe— king and man. You can be *all* the things. Lover and tease,' she whispered softly. 'Maybe husband and father even.'

His breathing roughened and he still couldn't steady his own heart. 'I don't know how to work it out. I don't know how to…'

'Maybe you don't have to. Not alone, not any more,' she said. 'Maybe we can figure it out together.'

He paused and his insides twisted. So did his lips in the slightest of smiles. 'Right. Together.'

'I don't expect you to have all the answers, Felipe. You might be a king, but you're not some kind of god.'

He'd have chuckled if he weren't still so terrified.

'You're just a man to me.' She stepped closer. 'But I do want you to be *my* man.'

'I am. You know I am.'

Elsie was beginning to know that, yes. Suddenly his arms snaked out and he pulled her close. For a long moment he crushed her to him. His face hard against her belly, his arms shaking with the strength to hold her as tight, as close as he could.

And feeling his surging emotion? She braced, her hands on his shoulders as a tumult of relief tore the loneliness apart. She was home and he was never letting her go.

'Elsie…'

'Can I help you with this?' She took hold of his crown and tugged it up.

'Oh. Yeah.' He'd clearly forgotten he even had the thing on. 'Thanks.'

She lifted it carefully and put it on the nearest table. When she turned back he was still on his knees, rubbing his temple where the crown had left a mark.

'What?' He registered her frown and a self-mocking expression crossed his face. 'Is the hat hair bad?'

'No. But that thing is horrendously heavy.'

'Real jewels,' he muttered.

'Yes.' Standing before him again, she gently ran her hands through his hair to ruffle it. He leaned in, closing his eyes when she pressed a little harder to massage his scalp.

'Better?' she asked softly.

'Yeah.' He caught her hand and drew the inside of her wrist to his mouth. His head still bowed, he stroked her skin so gently.

'You're so beautiful,' he said. 'Watching you play the mandolin in the café that day. It sounded so delicate, almost ethereal and you were like an angel come to make us feel…' He trailed off. 'And then last night I wanted to find something delicate but strong, something that shone as brilliantly as you so that when I had to watch you from far away, when I couldn't stand beside you, I would see it even from that distance. And I'd know that I'd offered and that you'd accepted something from me. That you'd chosen me.'

Her heart melted. The bracelet.

'It was too beautiful,' she muttered. 'And I was scared, Felipe. I didn't know how to handle it.'

'I can relate.' A flash of a smile, then he hesitated. 'Would you still say no?'

Never. Not now she knew just what he'd meant. And how much he'd meant it.

He reached into his pocket with his free hand. He still had it with him… Her blood scurried as he fastened the gleaming coil around her wrist—an unbreakable rope of diamonds linking her to him.

He looked at it for a moment and then lifted his gaze. She smiled tremulously as she read the shy pleasure in his eyes that she'd accepted his gift. This, a man who had everything, hadn't had the joy of giving before.

'I love you, Elsie. And I'd love you to stay. Please.'

'I have nothing to give you,' she said softly. 'Only me.'

'That's everything and all I'll ever need.'

He meant it. She saw how much he meant it in the

shimmering depths of his glistening eyes. Her legs gave out and she dropped to her knees to join him.

'I love you,' she whispered.

The kiss was messy and the tears wet and the laughter full of hiccups. But their hearts bloomed and the heat took over.

'How does this jacket even work?' She growled in frustration at the time taking to get to his skin.

He laughed a little and leaned back to divest himself of the jacket and everything else. Right there on the floor he stripped her too. And when she was naked and arching her hips he braced over her, locking her into the most delightful of cages.

'I know this is crazy quick,' he muttered. 'But I have no intention of rushing *this*. Not now.'

She trembled with the pleasure of being in his arms again. Of seeing the way he looked at her—with that adoration, relief, *joy* in his eyes.

'I didn't think I would ever have this again.' She gasped. 'You. Holding me.'

Tears then tumbled again, even in this sweetest, hottest of moments. But it was so intense. So desperately *wanted*. He held her through the storm, kissing her gently, staying with her—alongside her, inside her—as she released the last of that aching loss. And then he pressed closer, claiming his place in her body, her heart. And giving her his.

'Repeat after me,' he whispered. 'I belong to Felipe. And Felipe belongs to me.'

She smiled tremulously. 'I belong…'

Her eyes filled again and she couldn't finish it.

'I'm yours, Elsie,' he promised raggedly. 'And I'm never letting you go.'

'I never want you to,' she sobbed and clutched him closer still. 'I love you.'

They remained locked together for a long, long time after the searing cries of relief and of joy and of love had faded. It was an embrace she would never forget and never wanted to leave.

But eventually the worry machine that was her brain flicked back on.

'What are you thinking?' Felipe had felt her growing tension.

'They're going to say awful things about me,' she mumbled. 'Are you going to be able to handle it?'

'You're worried about me?'

She nodded. 'You—'

'Will not let them destroy anything.' He breathed in deeply. 'Nothing more of mine. I'm not losing you.'

'You won't,' she assured him. 'We can have time out. We can go down to the cave.'

His smile flashed. 'You like it?'

'Love it.'

'Me too.' He inhaled deeply. 'We'll get through it together. All of us.'

'All?'

'I talked to Amalia. You were right, I should have done that properly so much sooner. She would like to stay and go to school here in Silvabon.'

'And what would you like?'

'For her to stay.' He nodded.

'I'm so glad.'

Now his smile was sweet. 'So am I.'

There was a cautious knock on the door and an oddly high-pitched voice called, 'Your Majesty?'

Felipe groaned at the reminder, then laughed as he glanced at their total disarray. 'My aide is both frantic and terrified.'

'Your guests are waiting for you,' she said.

He nodded. 'I could send them all home?'

'No. You can't.' But she appreciated the offer. 'You need to go to the dinner.'

'Do you want to come with me?'

'Not this time. Not yet. Maybe I could have a tray in your room?' she suggested. 'I can wait for you there. Maybe I could stay a secret for a little while longer? Just while we…'

He gazed at her intensely. 'Are you okay with that?'

'Sure.' She suddenly grinned up at him. 'I might find some things to play with in there. I could shred your sheets and make a trapeze to swing from that balcony.'

He laughed. 'I'll be done with dinner in ten seconds.'

'No.' She turned serious again. 'They need time to celebrate with you. I get that you have a job to do. I'll be here and I'll figure out my own. With you. We have time on our side now, right?'

'We do.' His gaze turned smoky but he swiftly stood then held out his hand to help her up. 'Come on, I'll take you to my room now. I have to shower and change. Will you keep me company for that? I don't want to leave you even for a moment.'

'Is there a secret corridor to get from here to there?'

He flicked his eyebrows. 'Of course.'

Elsie smothered a giggle as she walked with her dishevelled, half-dressed king of a man along the curling, quiet corridor.

It had been barely one day—one day in which they'd found each other again, in which they'd felt and they'd fallen...

But now they had all the time in the world to be together. They had for ever.

CHAPTER NINETEEN

Two years later, 10.18 p.m.

TWENTY-FOUR HOURS COULD be a surprisingly long time. In twenty-four hours a man could fall in love. He could make life-changing vows. He could be driven crazy by the need to be alone with the love of his life and not be stuck in front of cameras live-streaming his every move to an audience of millions.

There'd been so *many* cameras. So many moments when he'd just wanted to tell the officiants to hurry the hell up. But there'd been protocols to follow, expectations to meet, and Felipe Roca de Silva y Zafiro was still working on that tricky thing known as work-life balance. But *now* time was his. And it was almost twenty-four hours since they'd last been alone. The wait had nearly killed him. And his new wife knew it.

Tightly gripping her hand, he led a softly chuckling Elsie along the narrowing tunnel. There was only one place he wanted to be and the fast route wasn't an option tonight. If she jumped into the ocean in that dress—and with the additional weight of the jewels in her necklace, earrings and tiara—she'd drown in seconds. He wasn't letting that happen.

'Spoilsport.'

She was still salty about it. Elsie had become quite the accomplished cliff jumper.

'You just want me to strip you sooner,' he countered playfully. 'Sorry, sweetheart, you're going to need just a little more patience.'

She shot him a sizzling look. Yeah, he knew her very well. Right now she was itching for him to undo the bajillion and one teeny tiny pearl buttons that fastened the demure lace back of her wedding gown. He was too—and she knew it. Which was why she was provoking him. He had, once again, left a ballroom of presidents and princes to party without him. Their wedding celebrations were still in full swing but he didn't give a damn. He was having his wedding night *now*. He'd waited long enough. And he definitely didn't have the patience for one button at a time.

'Felipe...'

She'd stopped just inside the secret doorway. He'd instructed his valet to make a few adjustments to their cave for the evening and it was worth it to see the look on her face the second she saw it.

More cushions, more rugs, scented candles as well—not just the chandeliers. There was food too—a spread of sumptuous delicacies in platters on a low table, easily accessible from the bed. Yes, there was an actual bed, swathed in soft white luxury linen. It was a four-poster and he had plans for those posts. And beside the bed there was a large ornately carved box. He'd put that there himself.

'What's in the box?'

He smiled, loving that it was the first thing she'd noticed.

'Silk ropes.'

'Silk…?' Her eyes went very round.

'And some other little things I think you might like.'

The colour in her cheeks was now very rosy. 'How long are you planning for us to stay down here?'

He pulled her close. 'At least twenty-four hours.'

Twenty-four hours could be a shockingly *long* time.

Elsie felt as if it had been for ever since she'd had Felipe alone and all to herself. She had something to tell him. Something important—she'd only found out herself late last night and because tradition dictated she couldn't see him again before the wedding she'd had to wait. But the wretched man distracted her—making her so mindless she couldn't even speak.

'Did you just rip the back of my wedding dress?' She gasped, giddy with excitement as he hauled her closer against his extremely hard body. 'Isn't it supposed to go on show in the palace later?'

'I'm sure someone can fix it,' he muttered.

He was fully a careless, spoilt king at that moment and she loved him for it. He knew what he wanted and he wanted it now. So did she.

'It's beautiful, by the way,' he growled. 'But can we get you out of it now?'

'Fel—'

Too late, he'd kissed her again and she was too far gone to remember her own name, let alone anything else. All she wanted was all of him. Their love-making was always pure energy, pure magic. But in this place—in his secret lair with its steaming mineral bath, on this, their wedding day—it was pure *heaven*.

'We're keeping the bed here,' he mused later when he'd recovered enough breath to speak. 'I can't believe I didn't think of it sooner.'

She rested her head on his chest, linking her fingers through his, and lifted their hands, admiring the way their wedding bands glinted in the light and her bracelet sparkled. 'Best honeymoon destination ever.'

He chuckled.

They'd weathered the storm of public scrutiny and judgement. He'd stood alongside her when the press had run story after story about her family. Felipe had kept her hand in his, kept her by his side, kept her head high and her heart full. And as he was the King who could do no wrong—they couldn't help noticing… *She obviously makes him happy.*

And she'd found her *own* focus—a deeply personal campaign of caring for the carers. She'd made under-the-radar visits to the local hospices, preparing food in the family accommodation for those supporting loved ones in hospitals, finding other ways to help them. Word had leaked—not from the palace—and while there'd been some nasty elements online, Elsie had kept up her visits and in fact done yet more. She wasn't going to let what people might say stop her from doing something that mattered so much to her. In this she *could* make a difference. A couple of patients' families had spoken out on her behalf, but it was the people she met personally who showed their appreciation. And that meant everything. As people on the street stood up for her, slowly the media opinion swivelled her way. Honestly that fact pleased Felipe more than it did her, but that he was so relieved for her? That made her smile.

'Amalia did such a great job today,' she murmured happily.

'Did you see some of the commentary online about her? She's just a child,' he grumbled.

'Felipe, she's almost sixteen.' Elsie chuckled. 'Don't let her hear you say that.' But Amalia had turned heads in her pretty bridesmaid's dress. 'They'll leave her alone while she's studying, won't they?'

'I'd like to hope so.' He sighed. 'It's good they've eased off on you.'

Amalia was attending her school locally, but she now had her heart set on attending a music conservatory abroad later. Composition was her jam—

she was fulfilling her artist's need to create. Elsie was creating something else entirely. She had to tell him. Now.

'Elsie?' He eased out from beneath her and rolled to his side so he could see her face. 'What are you thinking about?'

'That we're about to cause more scandal.'

'Oh?' He skimmed teasing fingertips across her belly.

'Correction.' She looked at him with a nervous smile. '*I* am about to cause more scandal.'

'Why, Elsie?' He pressed his mouth to the sensitive skin just beneath her belly button. 'What have you done?'

She shivered. Not from his kiss but because she was suddenly serious. Suddenly scared. 'The trolls are going to say I trapped you into marriage.'

'Trapped me? How?'

Elsie swallowed and lay very still. 'With the baby.'

He lifted his head. His eyes had darkened. And his palm was warm against her lower belly. 'Baby?'

'Yes.' Her eyes filled.

But his smile spread wide. 'Baby.'

'I think it was when we went on that secret trip to Italy and I told you I'd forgotten to bring my pills and that we needed to be careful.'

'But I wasn't careful.' He sounded so proud and so *smug* and he looked so gorgeously satisfied.

Suddenly her heart flew and her humour bubbled

up with it. 'You were so *reckless* we were almost caught by that ferry full of tourists!'

'And didn't that turn you on even more?' He laughed delightedly. 'Oh, Elsie!'

He was kissing her and she couldn't speak again. She could only cling to him as her own excitement and joy fought to find a way out of her limbs and into his.

'Given the wedding preparations have taken more than a year, I don't think the trolls' arguments will have any teeth. If they only knew the truth...' he muttered between kisses. 'If only, if only...'

'The truth?'

He ran his hand down her body with the surest, most possessive touch yet. 'That I'm the one who's trapped you. That here I am holding you prisoner in my personal dungeon and I even plan to tether you to my bed.'

Her breathing shortened. '*Tether* me?'

'Right now, as it happens.'

'Now?' She wriggled in an automatic response to the surge of electricity his words had charged within her.

'So you can't distract me while I show you just how much I love you. So you can't escape from the truth of how much you've changed my life. I'm going to thank you, Elsie. I'm going to please you.' He pulled a strip of silk from that ornate box at the side of the bed. 'Is that okay with you?'

'Uh…' Breathless already, she licked her lips. 'Yes. But *I'm* going to explore that box later…'

'I hope so.' He carefully wrapped the silks around her wrists, his smile tender and possessive. 'I can't wait to meet our baby.' His voice quietened as he worked. As he was honest and vulnerable with her. 'Part of me is terrified. I'm desperate to protect her. But I know that with you…we can do this. Together.'

'Yes.'

Felipe had pushed forward with relinquishing some of the Crown's more substantial powers and he'd formulated a new succession plan that had been put to a public vote. His people had supported him entirely. So now their little prince or princess would become heir to the Crown only when old enough to understand the decision. There would be *choice* and more privacy in their children's lives.

His gaze down her body was intense and brooding and so, so fierce. 'I want this baby with you,' he breathed. 'I want lots of babies with you. I want everything with you.'

'Especially more holidays, right?'

'Yes.' He chuckled. 'Holidays and babies and laughter and you always with me on public engagements and so much time alone together down here. I love you, Elsie. Don't ever leave me.'

'I love you,' Elsie whispered, every bit as fierce and emotional and honest. 'And I never will.'

She was locked in his love and he in hers.

If they'd been looking they might've glimpsed

the bright flashes of colour from the celebratory fireworks through the narrow gap in the rocks. But they weren't looking.

They were too busy detonating fireworks of their own.

* * * * *

Couldn't get enough of
The Night the King Claimed Her?
Don't miss these other stories by
Natalie Anderson!

Secrets Made in Paradise
The Queen's Impossible Boss
Stranded for One Scandalous Week
Nine Months to Claim Her
Revealing Her Nine-Month Secret

Available now!